Serious Trouble

ILLINOIS SHORT FICTION

A list of books in the series appears at the end of this volume.

Paul Friedman

Serious Trouble

UNIVERSITY OF ILLINOIS PRESS

Urbana and Chicago

Publication of this work was supported in part by a grant from the Illinois Arts Council, a state agency.

The author wishes to thank the MacDowell Colony, the Ossabaw Island Project, and the Center for Advanced Study at the University of Illinois for providing time and place.

Manufactured in the United States of America
C 5 4 3 2 1

This book is printed on acid-free paper.

"Blackburn," *Cimarron Review,* no. 68, July 1984

"The Family," *Mid-American Review,* vol. 2, no. 2, Fall 1982; winner of the *MAR* 1983 Sherwood Anderson Prize for Short Fiction

Library of Congress Cataloging-in-Publication Data

Friedman, Paul, 1937–
Serious trouble.

(Illinois short fiction)
I. Title. II. Series.
PS3556.R54S4 1986 813'.54 85-28843
ISBN 0-252-01310-7 (alk. paper)

To the memory of my grandmother,

Mary Punia (1877–1970),

and to

Dale Seidel (1952–83)

Contents

An Unexpected Death

Raleigh Bauer told his wife, Donna, that he was going out on the porch. It was a quarter to ten on a Saturday morning at the end of March. The local newspaper, the *Penfield Journal*, lay on the bottom step with a rubber band around it.

Though the radio said it was seventy-two at the airport, it felt almost hot to Raleigh. He looked up at a cloudless sky. This was the kind of day everyone had been waiting for and, if the forecast was right, it would be warmer still the next few days, and dry.

He noticed Cheryl across the street in the Flessner driveway hosing the VW. Damn, had he known how skimpy that bathing suit was he'd have checked on the weather sooner. Her father, Chick, was in the sideyard clear on the other side of their house, pacing.

Donna came to the doorway. "You want some coffee?"

That would make three cups. As he said yes it crossed his mind this would be a good time to set the martin house up in the backyard, but he wasn't really ready to get his day underway and knowing Donna he knew she wouldn't get on him if he never put it up. That was just the way Donna was.

"I'll get it. Come on out here and sit down," Raleigh said, getting to his feet.

"It's no bother," Donna said, "stay where you are." But before she'd gone more than a few steps Raleigh had the storm door open.

"*Donna!*" As she turned he let fly with the tee-shirt that he'd just taken off. She raised her hands and grabbed it shoulder high.

"*All right*," he said, "good catch."

Donna didn't say a thing at first, just stood in the hall with the shirt in her hand. Then she slowly cocked her head to one side. "Look at you. You know, I think you're getting fat."

They'd been married twenty-four years. His Popeye tattoo, which he'd gotten on East Main Street in Shit City—Norfolk, Virginia—was fading and blurred on his right forearm; lines that were dark and deeply etched cut across his forehead, but his weight had varied very little through the years.

"No way."

"And look at this." She was pointing out a hole in his shirt.

It was, he said, the only one he'd had in his drawer.

"Then we better go out to Sears one night and get you some underwear and stuff."

Donna walked off without another word, leaving Raleigh standing in the hall by himself.

He was six feet even, red haired, and usually quick to smile. His hands, which he was now staring down at, were pretty good sized and even though he didn't use them to earn his living anymore, there were thick callouses on them. Up to this point he hadn't ever been in anything but good health.

Back on the porch Raleigh thumbed through the paper without really seeing the words he was looking at. For some months now things had been edging in on him; that was the feeling, anyway, and he didn't understand it. He'd been unsettled by thoughts that were so fleeting he couldn't put words to them, yet they'd leave him feeling in need of some kind of reassurance. Finally an ad on the inside page of the sports section caught his attention. The ad had appeared in yesterday's paper too.

PUBLIC INVITED FREE SEMINAR
How To Wake Up To The FINANCIAL GENIUS
Inside You

When Donna returned he pointed it out, as he had last night.

"You're just bound and determined to go to that, aren't you?"

"I wouldn't say that but I have to decide pretty soon."

The seminar was being held from noon to 1:30 at the Penfield Motor Inn. Raleigh suspected this free seminar would be half a bubble off plumb, still he wouldn't mind hearing what they had to say. For awhile now he'd been thinking in a kind of vague way that he ought to know more about the very things that were listed in the ad: everything from how to legally lower your taxes to how to go about ensuring a bright financial future for yourself. He wasn't sure, of course, if this would be of any help. Everything seemed to revolve around real estate.

"No one there's going to rip me off," he said. "I don't worry about that part of it."

In fact, financially Raleigh had done better than a whole lot of people. With his wife and family he'd been living on Sanford Drive for ten years now, which wasn't too shabby as far as Raleigh was concerned.

Donna looked halfway distracted for a moment. "Is that Larry?" she asked, and before Raleigh could answer she turned to go back in.

"Morning, Dad. Man, fresh air and sunshine. I don't know if I can handle this." Larry handed Raleigh the glasses he was supposed to use for reading. "Hey, Cheryl's home."

Disregarding that, Raleigh asked his nineteen-year-old son, who now played electric guitar with a rock and roll band that had formed a couple of months earlier, how it had gone last night.

"Not too bad. We had a real good crowd. Tiny is pretty sure they're going to ask us to play there again."

"You boys must be pretty good."

"We're getting there. I guess Mom wrote back to Scott," Larry said, "didn't she? I saw the envelope laying on the table."

Raleigh nodded. "We didn't feel like we could put it off."

Yesterday a letter from Larry's older brother, Scott, had arrived, in which he told them he was extending his enlistment.

"Scott must have weirded out, that's all I can say. I sure hope he knows what he's doing."

Raleigh nodded. He'd been a disbursing clerk when he'd been in the navy and he knew exactly what his son Scott was doing. Extending for a year would increase the reenlistment bonus he'd receive when he shipped over, and if he made first class during the extension, and if he shipped for six years, not just four, then right about a year from now when he'd probably do it—reenlist—he's have himself a heck of a payday.

"I think I'll go over and say hello to Cheryl."

"Sure. Go on."

If Scott really was planning on making a career of the navy, Raleigh thought, this was the first any of them knew of it.

Across the street Cheryl played a stream of water in Larry's direction.

Raleigh remembered that back when he'd been a short-timer he couldn't wait to get out. He'd been discharged at Pensacola and he could still remember spending his first night on the beach as a civilian, getting liquored up with a couple of guys off the *Driscoll* who he'd been in DK school with in Newport. But hell, that was it. After that he went on home where Donna Schultz, the girl he'd gone with all through high school, had been as ready as he was to get married. She'd been a secretary at Dreiser Tent & Awning at the time and within two months of his discharge he was pounding nails, a carpenter apprentice. Not too long afterward Scott came along, then there was Larry.

Construction had been booming and he spent six years, starting in 1969, working on P.L.&E.'s nuclear power plant at Gibson. That was the sweetest tit he'd had up to that time: $18.50 an hour the day that he began with two bucks an hour more on the second shift, but Raleigh never fooled himself. At Gibson you spent half your time hanging off the wall; anything could happen. Someone might see a live wire arcing at 900 Control; electricians would want carpenters to go up there to build a platform for them. A rigging crew would have to fly the lumber in, and hairy as it was scabbing that platform together, there were times when it was just as hairy being down below. You'd hear someone holler "headache," which meant that someone way the hell above you had dropped his hammer or his wrench and if you were underneath it that was it but you didn't bitch too much, the wages were too good, and then as the job at Gibson wound down Harold, his brother-in-law, who ran commercials on TV and took out full-page ads in the Sunday *Journal*—he operated a siding company that was fair-to-middling-sized by downstate standards—asked him to come aboard.

Siding and storms, drains and gutters, roofing: "We're part of weatherization," Harold said, "it's a growth industry."

That sounded good to Raleigh; he'd been ready for a change and he signed on.

You think you know what you're doing, Raleigh thought. You think you're making a smart move. Oh hell—he turned and called through the open door, "Donna, you doing anything right now? Come on outside for a while."

"I'm making out the shopping list. Would you ask Larry if he wants pancakes?"

"He's busy. You might as well close the kitchen up," Raleigh said.

The territory he was going over was territory he'd gone over many times before. Raleigh wasn't in the habit of searching out or mulling over the events of his life, of making assessments, but feeling as he did he could hardly afford to disregard anything. Was he a success, he wondered, because he didn't feel that he was even though he knew that by most standards he'd done fairly well, which made him wonder how much of this was his own doing, something purely in his mind.

Chick started across the street. It almost seemed, Raleigh thought, as if he wanted some kind of a fresh start, then his train of thought was broken when he realized Chick was approaching.

"How you doing?"

"Oh, pretty good. I don't think weather comes much better than this."

"Not around here it doesn't." Raleigh invited Chick to sit down.

Their acquaintanceship had never amounted to anything much. As Chick put his sunglasses on, then climbed the steps, about all that came to Raleigh's mind in terms of their recent past was a picture of Chick's wife, Barbara, standing in his living room collecting for some charity.

Chick, who worked at the Merrill Lynch office in Sunnybrook Plaza, refereed high school football games. He was wearing plaid slacks, the kind Raleigh associated with people who kept a golf bag in the trunk of their car.

"No," Raleigh said, "more weather like this sure won't be too hard to take."

"Heck of a winter though," Chick said.

"Lord." Raleigh shook his head. Then Chick asked about his family. "Oh, can't complain. Wouldn't do any good if I did, would it?"

"Probably not." Chick made no further effort at conversation.

Neither did Raleigh, who blew his nose then let his gaze drift until it settled on the pair across the street. They seemed to have plenty to say to each other. Chick's girl, Cheryl, had a definite height advantage.

Barely five feet seven, his son Larry never had played sports and as for his long hair Raleigh agreed with Donna when she said so long as he kept it neat and clean his hair was his concern. From time to time Larry said he might apply to Armstrong Community College. Raleigh would believe it when he saw it. He thought of Larry mainly as a dreamer, and when he and Donna would talk about this son, who bused tables at the Enterprise, he found that he really couldn't put his finger on his feelings.

Seeing Chick looking in Cheryl and Larry's direction Raleigh said, "They sure grow up fast, don't they?"

"Do they ever," Chick said. "Too fast. Too damn fast."

Suddenly a wave of emotion swept over Raleigh. He brought his hand to his face. It took awhile before he turned to Chick, who could have noticed something, Raleigh worried, but Chick had taken his sunglasses off and was rubbing both his eyes with his fists, which relieved Raleigh and he was relieved because the feeling he'd been swept by had passed; nevertheless, things were not exactly as they had been. A change had taken place. Like someone who'd suffered a scare, Raleigh was now glad to have company and it didn't matter if the company was talkative or not.

"You happen to watch the news on Channel 6 last night?"

"No, I don't think I did."

"You missed it," Raleigh said. "A preacher over in Cissna Park was claiming the world would end in the next ninety days. And he's got some damn fools in his church believing him."

"In Cissna Park? Hell," Chick said, "I thought the Dutch had more sense than that."

"I guess not. People in this church put their land up for sale. They're supposed to head for Missouri to wait it out over there."

"I grew up in Bellweather," Chick said. "That's about thirty miles east of Cissna."

"I've heard of it but I've never been there."

Donna came out.

"Oh, Chick, hi."

"I was just telling Chick about that preacher on the news last night. Wasn't he something?"

She nodded. "But that's about all you ever get on the news anymore. Either there's a wreck or someone's been murdered or some preacher's telling you the world is coming to an end. I swear," she sighed, then she turned to Chick. "When's Barbara getting back?"

"Couple of days I suppose. Her mother's not doing too well."

"Oh, the poor thing."

"I guess it's just a matter of time," Chick said, and when he turned to Raleigh, Raleigh shook his head to show that he sympathized.

He knew that Barbara taught in the junior high, but he hadn't known she wasn't home. Donna had, and though it wasn't fair to sit here and be irritated because she hadn't mentioned this to him, it was irritating him.

"Raleigh," Donna said, "where's Larry?"

"Over there with Cheryl," Raleigh said, moving his head to indicate the direction, but then he saw that Larry wasn't there, which startled him. The driveway was completely empty.

"I think they went inside the house," Chick said.

"Oh, is Cheryl home for the weekend?" Donna asked.

"Well, let's just say she's home." Chick paused. "She's not going to school anymore. Barbara doesn't even know about this yet."

Sometimes you couldn't win for losing, Raleigh thought. He saw the VW was inside the damn garage. Across the street the front door opened.

Cheryl came out. She'd changed from her bathing suit into a baseball top and blue jeans. Then his son, who'd been wearing nothing on his head when he'd gone across the street, appeared with a bright orange headband on and Raleigh didn't like what he was seeing. In fact the headband, as it combined with hair that fell to the shoulders, came across as evidence, yet no else seemed to notice that something very wrong could be going on.

"They sure don't make it easy on us old folks," Donna said.

Raleigh tried not to be abrupt.

"I guess it's a hard time for kids too," Chick said, "you know. At least that's what I keep trying to tell myself."

"Well," Raleigh said to his neighbor as he stood, "time for me to do some work." Then he turned to Donna. "I'm going inside." He turned once more to Chick. "Take her easy."

Midstate Siding's Penfield office was down in Raleigh's basement. The main office was south of Penfield in Bloomington, where Harold lived. Downstairs the first thing Raleigh did was kick the bottom drawer of his metal filing cabinet shut. Son of a bitch.

He turned the dehumidifier on then called Pick Loomis, who'd sometimes do some guttering for Midstate. Next, in an album he showed potential customers, Raleigh mounted a couple of before and after photographs of properties Midstate had sided and after that, back upstairs again, he changed clothes and called, "I'm leaving." Still upset, he didn't wait for an answer.

But by the time he was behind the wheel of his gray Electra a shift had taken place. Now he was upset with himself. You don't do the kind of thing he'd just done and then forget it.

He knew why he'd almost stomped off. Because Larry and Cheryl's messing around had gotten to him, but Chick hadn't been shook up and Donna didn't seem to think that anything out of line was going on. It went back to the same damn thing: he wasn't exactly himself anymore, and if more proof was needed all he had to do was look at the irritation he'd been feeling toward Donna.

They ought to go away together for a couple of days, he thought, just the two of them. Then he started having second thoughts. He took a left. She'd need a reason. He drove past an empty parking lot. Talk about pitiful, he thought. Ever since the damn city council took to improving downtown, things had gone from bad to worse. They blocked off the main street and turned downtown into an outdoor mall. Doing something just to be doing something. Hell, wasn't that the way it always was? The only difference the damn mall made was now imitation gas lamps were all over the place and it took you some extra time to get wherever you were going. While waiting for a red light on Chambers, Raleigh felt his lips move. Then there was a sudden flash of light, which turned out to be the sun reflecting off the bubble window of a van crossing right in front of him.

Well, was he going to go to that seminar or not? It would be easy to shoot the seminar down, but then again, if he didn't go he'd wonder if he wasn't passing something up. That was the dilemma and it continued until he came to Vine and Matthews, which was only half a block from his first stop.

Instead of worrying, he thought as he stepped from his car into the sunlight, do something.

"Looking good." Raleigh's tone was practiced.

His applicator, Smitty, who was on a walkboard putting backer on the north side of this two-story frame house called, Hold on, he'd be right down.

"Take your time." Raleigh started off around the house. Maybe it was because he was feeling warm, but it seemed to Raleigh that if this was his place he'd put a shade tree in out front, even though Crawford's lilac bush and redbud were a heck of a lot better than that damn junk tree those folks across the street had, the Tree of Heaven.

Shit, he thought, no one liked going around unnerved half the time, which was what it amounted to. Then while he was standing in the sideyard, Vern, the kid who worked along with Smitty, came over and asked if he had a light.

"No. I sure don't."

"That's okay. I think there's matches in the truck."

Raleigh liked the wide paved driveway. It gave the place a squared-away appearance. There was some lumber laying in the yard next door, and when Raleigh went over he saw that sure enough those 1-by-12s nearest to the garage didn't have a knot in them. That grade pine cost as much as most hardwoods anymore, but hell, he could see it, look at Midstate, they never used anything but top-of-the-line material, which was one reason why they didn't have to hand out the kind of fluky guarantee that wasn't worth the paper it was written on the way some of those hammer-and-truck operations did.

By the time Raleigh had worked his way back to Smitty, Smitty had come down and was bending over a hose.

"You're going to have to do some channeling back where that pipe runs up from the basement."

"Could be," Smitty said. "Man, you lucked out. When Crawford came out and saw we took the trim off he like to had a damn fit. He said you never said a damn thing to him about us taking that off."

"Hell I didn't." Raleigh toed the ground; Smitty didn't say a word. Then Vern returned with an old man in tow.

"Here's the man you want to talk to," Vern said.

The gray-haired man, who was carrying a sack of groceries, approached.

"Yes sir. What can I do for you?" Raleigh asked.

"That your sign out front?"

"Sure is," Raleigh said. "Here, let's set those groceries down." They walked over to Crawford's picnic table. "I'm Raleigh Bauer."

"Clarence Knapp." The old man said he was starting to think siding just might be the way to go and Raleigh agreed. Then he and Mr. Knapp watched as Smitty and Vern started back to work.

"From what I hear aluminum siding's pretty darn durable stuff."

"I reckon you know the homeowner here's getting steel."

"Steel? Well I'll be darned. That's a new one on me. Doesn't seem like steel would look right on a house."

"Yeah it does."

Mr. Knapp didn't argue. "Once you put siding on I guess you never have to mess with painting again."

"That's about right."

"Then by golly if the price wasn't too steep I don't know how a guy could beat it."

"Heck, don't let price stop you. We can most generally work that out." The old man was receptive, Raleigh thought. "Tell you what. How about us setting up a time for me to look at your house. That way I could show you exactly what we have to offer."

"I believe I'll hold off on that," the old man said. Then he turned to gather up his sack of groceries.

And Raleigh acknowledged what he already knew, what he'd known ever since he first set eyes on that ad: that he'd be going to the seminar.

Mr. Knapp started for the sidewalk. Raleigh walked along with him.

"Here I'd been thinking we'd have a cold spring," the old man said.

"We still might, changeable as the weather's been," Raleigh said in front of the house. "You might as well take one of these." He handed the old man his business card. "You be sure and keep us in mind now."

The old man said he would and crossed the street. When Raleigh returned he gave Vern and Smitty the thumbs up sign.

"You boys are passing up something good if you don't canvass this neighborhood," he said. There was an eight-percent commission involved, but neither Vern nor Smitty answered. "Well," Raleigh finally said, "I see I'm running kind of late. On a tight schedule."

"Must be nice," Smitty said.

Raleigh laughed. "You boys hang in there now."

He made a few more stops then drove to the dank six-story parking garage across the street from the Penfield Motor Inn.

The people here would be just like him, he imagined: wanting to do better. You couldn't fault anyone for that.

Standing in front of a urinal in the men's room on the eleventh floor, Raleigh couldn't remember what his own boys had looked like when they'd been six and seven, which was right about the age of the youngster he'd just seen on the elevator. The youngster had had a sheriff's badge pinned on his shirt and he'd been wearing a two-holster gun belt.

A man standing a couple of urinals down looked over. "Sure is hot in here," he said, shaking his head, making his breath whistle.

"What happened to the air conditioning?" Raleigh said.

"I think they forgot to run a duct in here, don't you."

"Is that it?"

Raleigh went over to the basin and pressed the soap dispenser. It was 20 after twelve. He was half wishing he'd gotten off the elevator on the eighth floor and gone to King's for a fish sandwich. Instead, out in the corridor, he turned away from Conference Room C and, after a slight hesitation, moved toward the Tip Top Room, a lounge and piano bar where, according to the poster, the Fairlanes were appearing nightly.

He pushed through the swinging doors. It was dark in here; there was plush carpeting. Deep red booths lined the wall. The bartender, a college-age kid in a white shirt and red vest, came over and Raleigh asked for a Michelob Light. Then he dug some loose change out of his pocket and slowly turned around on the stool. The only other person was a woman sitting at the end of the bar.

When the bartender came back with Raleigh's beer he set a dish of popcorn down in front of him.

"I thought you might get a crowd from that seminar they're holding down the hall," Raleigh said.

"We sure didn't." The bartender seemed to think about it. "Are you talking about that reunion of World War II vets I heard was going on?"

"No. This is real estate."

"Real estate. I'll be darned."

Funny as he was feeling about going to this seminar, there surely hadn't been any need for him to be the one to bring it up. Yet he went on.

"They'll probably lay out the do's and don't's."

"Sounds good."

"Shit. I'll bet you anything you want it's just another one of those get-rich-quick schemes you're always hearing about."

The bartender narrowed his eyes and nodded slowly.

"But just like the ad in the paper says. The only investment they're asking us to make is two hours' time. Hell, I can afford that."

"You can give them that much, can't you?"

"Randy," the woman called, "are you going to tell me what page the good parts are on? I'm not going through this whole damn book." She motioned with the paperback.

The bartender walked to the end of the bar. Raleigh drained his glass and pushed it forward.

"What's that called?" he asked a few minutes later as the bartender mixed the woman's drink.

"Your basic watermelon is what it is. Sweet as the dickens but Marlene likes them. It's vodka and strawberry liqueur."

Marlene gave no indication she knew she was being talked about. When her drink came she took it and went to the jukebox.

Then the bartender returned to the conversation. "Yes sir, if someone's looking to make big bucks I'd have to say this probably is not the place to be. No one's told me how to do it, anyway," he said and laughed, and Raleigh laughed along with him. Then the bartender asked Raleigh what kind of work he did.

"Midstate Siding," Raleigh said, taking out his card, which the bartender picked up.

"Things slowing down any? The reason I ask is, my Dad lives in Danville and it's getting bad there."

"It's getting bad all through this part of the state."

"I saw in the paper where Allis Chalmers laid off 300 people," Randy said. "And the Cahill plant out west of town shut down. They made parts for John Deere."

"Are you from Danville?"

"Ludlow."

"Ludlow. You wouldn't know Oren Coombes, would you?"

"Hell, I worked with his youngest boy, John."

"I'll be darned."

"Talk about a god-awful job," Randy said. "Me and John worked for Duster Simmons. He's county road commissioner. Work your butt off in the winter keeping the roads clear and the rest of the time you oil them or haul gravel. That gets old real fast."

Raleigh nodded then realized he knew the song that was playing. It was *Rock Around the Clock*. This wouldn't happen but once in a hundred times and when the woman came over and asked the bartender to turn the jukebox up, Raleigh said, "That song's been around a mighty long time, you know it?"

"I love it," she said. "It's my all-time favorite. Bill Haley and the Comets recorded it," she hesitated, "let's see," she looked up at the ceiling fan, "twenty-seven years ago."

"Is that right?"

Automatically Raleigh subtracted to see how old he'd been back then: forty-four less twenty-seven. He'd been seventeen. This was a habit he'd somehow fallen into, and as if to complete the process he now added the numbers: forty-four plus twenty-seven. Seventy-one. That didn't seem real. In the same number of years that had gone by since *Rock Around the Clock* had come out he'd be seventy-one. Thinking about it that way made becoming seventy-one something that would happen to him made being seventy-one something that actually wasn't all that far away.

Marlene was looking at him. He smiled back but she wasn't smiling and she didn't turn away. She held his eyes until, in some confusion, he looked away. He looked down and fumbled for his wallet.

"Randy," Raleigh called. He lay two dollar bills on the bar. "Give Marlene another watermelon when she's ready," he said. Then he finished off his beer and pushed away from the bar.

"Thanks," she said, making a gesture with her glass as if to toast him.

He could hardly look at her.

"Time for me to be going," he said.

"Mother waiting on you, is she?" Marlene asked.

"That's about right."

Just keep walking Raleigh thought as he pushed through the swinging doors. Son of a bitch, this wasn't his day. He followed the narrow winding corridor but went in the wrong direction and had to double back to get to Conference Room C, where he stood in front of the door. Talk about feeling dumb and embarrassed: he couldn't have come across as more of a fool if he tried, he thought, walking in. A couple of people who were already seated watched as he made his way to one of the contoured chairs in the middle of this horseshoe-shaped room. Since it couldn't be undone just see it for what it was, he told himself, don't blow it out of proportion but sitting down he thought Son of a bitch, this really wasn't his day. He stretched his legs and crossed his arms, then noticed the small recessed lights that were sprinkled all over the ceiling.

Forty-four years old and what he saw made him want to laugh. Up at the front of the room the table between the speaker's stand and the free-standing blackboard gave it away. It had books and magazines and tapes on it even though the speaker himself wasn't here yet. That was about as blatant as you could get.

Then he made the connection. This room reminded him of the ready room on the *Leyte*, not that he could remember being in it all that many times since the ready room had been back in officers' country but when he'd first reported aboard he'd been assigned to X Division and that's where they'd gone for orientation. The *Leyte: CVS 32:* she'd long since been mothballed. She'd been about the last of the straight deck carriers. *Essex* class, anti-submarine warfare. They operated off the Atlantic coast, not like the *Forrestal* with its angled deck and two-runway system which made a Med cruise every year. Missing out on those cruises to the Med had probably saved him a couple of trips to the clapshack Raleigh thought as he looked around the room, which was only about a quarter full when the speaker came in a few minutes later. There were three or four young couples, some people who looked retired, and then half a row of boys about college age but that was it with the exception of a scattering of folks who, like him, were sitting off by themselves.

The speaker, who was about thirty-five and wearing a banker's blue suit and vest, tousled the hair of a youngster who belonged to one of the couples then checked the display on the table and went to the stand.

"Could I get you folks to move down and sit a little closer together?"

As other people rose from their seats and moved Raleigh decided he would stay in his seat. His expression became thoughtful, distant; it looked as if he was a thousand miles away. And that expression remained until everyone had settled down.

Raleigh saw what was going on. It was his intention to resist everything. Why *am* I here, he wondered. He looked at his watch. It was twenty to one. He'd give himself a certain amount of time to listen to this—maybe half an hour—then by God he was leaving.

"I'm pleased to be with you today, ladies and gentlemen," the speaker said, smiling and looking around. "My name is Glen Fitzgerald and I'm here representing Doug Emerson. Ladies and gentlemen, I think this will be a profitable afternoon for all of us so without any further delay let me put the central question of the day to you. Is it still possible, in this day and age, to go from almost nothing to financial freedom in a relatively brief period of time? Doug Emerson says that it is. That's why he's sponsoring these seminars all across the country. You may have seen Doug on the *Today* show, or he might be familiar to you because his picture's been in the pages of some of the country's best-known magazines. Nationally known as a writer and lecturer, Doug happens to be a self-made millionaire, and now he wants you to learn the money making techniques that worked so successfully for him.

"Before we go any further let's clear up one thing. I'm not here to sell you another high-priced seminar. Second, let's make sure we have our priorities straight.

"Each and every one of us is mighty important."

His voice dropped; he spaced his words and spoke with intensity. "I am a unique event, ladies and gentlemen, never to be repeated, and so are you. I believe each and every one of us is as priceless as any painting by the famous artist Leonardo da Vinci. And because of that," he said, "because each one of us is unique"—his eyes took in the entire room—"some of us will succeed and some will fail, but now I'm getting ahead of myself.

"Before we talk about succeeding, let's talk about survival. What do we need just to survive?" He repeated the question, then went to the blackboard and picked up a piece of chalk. "What do we need for basic physical survival?"

Someone called "Oxygen."

"Oxygen. Good." He wrote "Air" on the board. "We have to breathe if we're going to survive. Anything else?"

"How about food?"

"Let's say water. Okay, air, water—. Are we leaving something out?"

"Shelter."

"There you go." He wrote down "Shelter" then returned to the stand and went on. "When you're talking about survival you're talking about shelter and when you're talking about shelter you're talking about real estate. Does everyone agree?"

Though no one said yes out loud, people were nodding their heads. "I don't believe anyone's going to argue with me when I say that makes real estate a pretty attractive investment. Necessities are not likely to go out of style. Of course the prophets of doom and gloom will tell you gold's the way to go and the big money boys say put your money in the stock market and I guess if you know enough about antique snuff boxes or Chinese ceramics you stand a chance of making a profit from the craze in collectibles but ladies and gentlemen I submit to you that looked at on a historical basis you'll see investments in homes and rental properties have doubled in value and doubled again in the post-war era. We've seen the value in real estate increase by the month, and could you ever come up with a more reassuring testimonial that this: investments in rental properties have not only kept up with, they've far outpaced the rate of inflation."

He paused, then spoke very soberly.

"We're living in inflationary times. Nowadays inflation is a fact of life. Of course you folks don't need me to tell you that, but I would like to take this opportunity to clear up some misconceptions about inflation. Excuse the language, ladies, but I've had people say to me, Glen, inflation scares the living H out of me. Well I'm here to tell you that inflation doesn't add to or take away from wealth. What it does is *rearrange* wealth, which means some folks will prosper and some will suffer, and it's my personal belief that whether you prosper or suffer is up to you.

"Ladies and gentlemen, you hold your financial destiny in your own hands. The controlling factor isn't inflation. It's not your current bank balance or your track record either. No sir, it's—does anyone know what I'm going to say?" There was silence. "The controlling factor is"—he hesitated—"attitude. That's right. Let me say it again. Attitude." He nodded his head then raised his arm and checked his watch.

"I believe we started a few minutes late and we're still running behind so if you'll hold off any questions you might have I'll move right along and then we'll take a short break but first, with your permission, ladies and gentlemen, I'd like to tell you about a man who in the period of two hours time lost both his home and his business. When I saw this young man he was crying, ladies and gentlemen, weeping like a baby, but you'll understand when I tell you he was weeping tears of joy because the day I'm talking about was back in 1976—that terrible day the Teton Dam burst and a twenty-foot wall of water roared through Rapid City, South Dakota, sweeping away most everything in its path. When I saw this young man I'm telling you about he'd just learned that his family was safe. The good Lord had seen fit to spare his wife and two children. So you see," the speaker said, and now he paused, "it's no wonder the tears he was shedding were tears of thanksgiving." He paused once again. "Attitude, ladies and gentlemen, that's what it's all about." Glen took a drink of water.

This guy was slicker than a whistle, Raleigh thought. Here he was listening to this b.s. when he could be somewhere else doing something worthwhile. Raleigh imagined himself out in the backyard putting up his martin house, but then he knew exactly what he felt like doing. He could be home with Donna right now fooling around. There you go,

Raleigh thought. Actually the only reason he was here was because once he got something in his mind it was near impossible for him to shake it. Stubbornness was what it was.

"Ma'am, what kind of car do you drive?" Glen was looking at a woman in the front row. Raleigh missed her answer. "Well, what kind of car would you like to drive?" The man sitting beside the woman nudged her and she laughed, but if she answered Raleigh didn't hear it. "Well, how would a silver-blue Mercedes suit you? The 450 SL. That's the kind of machine that just about makes you drool, isn't it? Let's imagine for a minute that the dealer here in Penfield is holding a promotion. He's giving one away. You go down to the showroom and fill out the forms then you don't think another thing about it until a week later when you get a call saying they held the drawing and guess what, you won. Of course you can't believe it but you go to the showroom and by God the manager hands you the keys. It's really yours. You actually drive this beautiful machine home. You've never been so proud of anything in all your life. For two weeks you don't do anything but baby it, then you decide to take it out in the country for a drive."

People in the room were eating this up, Raleigh thought. It almost seemed like they came here to let their imaginations run wild. Not him. He still wished he was home with Donna but he couldn't just get up and walk out. Instead he thought back to the *Leyte*, how after days of water hours and general quarters all hands would come down with channel fever the night before they were due back in port. She'd been a feeder though.

". . . you're being super-careful," Glen was saying, "when you see a boy standing in the middle of the road. You slow up and when he doesn't move you go to steer around him. That's when you notice he has a rock in his hand. He rears back and you know some folks will do most anything these days just to tear something up but even so you can't believe it when he lets loose of that big old rock and it smacks against your hood. The windshield shatters. You slam on your brakes, jump out." Glen paused to gain the full effect. "Now tell me something, ma'am, would you? What's your attitude? What do you want to do to that boy?"

"Kill him," the man sitting next to the woman said, and the people in the room burst into laughter.

"Right," Glen said. Then suddenly his tone changed. "Until you notice that the little fellow's nose is bloody, until you see he's crying, until he says, I'm sorry lady but I had to make you stop. We had an accident. My Dad's hurt real bad." Glen looked out at the people in the room. "That would change everything, wouldn't it?"

"Attitude." He nodded his head as if that one word said it all. Then he leaned forward and when he spoke his voice was filled with emotion. "The little boy in that story did what he had to do and so should everyone of you. Ladies and gentlemen, get into real estate now, during this downturn. There's never going to be a better time to do it. There's opportunity in adversity. Think of yourselves as winners." He waited, wiped his forehead, and straightened up to his full height. His voice was normal when he spoke again.

"We don't recommend raw land. There's no liquidity there. And commercial property is too closely tied to the economic cycle for that to be a good investment. No, Doug recommends you go the residential route. The first thing to do is narrow the possibilities down, create a window. Specialize in single-family dwellings, duplexes, apartment houses, that's up to you. Then you want to learn the market in your area. Here's a rule of thumb: never go more than half an hour from your own home when you're looking at properties. Your time is important, ladies and gentlemen, and remember this: bargains can be had anywhere."

Then without warning, as if something had occurred to him that he had to consider, Glen stopped talking. While the people in the room, who'd been hanging on his every word, waited, Raleigh remembered standing on a deck-edge catwalk at night watching arresting cables snare S2F's and AD5's as they came in over the bow and landed on the *Leyte's* outlined flight deck. That had been a heck of a thing for a kid to see. The navy had given him a ton of memories. He remembered being in his rack then racing topside; the bitchbox woke him: *General quarters, general quarters. This is not a drill.* He was hose man on a damage control team, but when he reached the flight deck he saw there wasn't any getting to the locker where the gear was stowed. No one seemed to know what to do. In the disbursing office the next morning he and Chief Hanson had closed out the pay records of the men who'd died the night before. Coming in for a landing an S2F had lost the hook, climbed the barrier, and slammed into the island. Christ, how many people had bought it in the photo lab? He couldn't even remember anymore.

Glen was gearing up to speak. It looked as if he'd come to a difficult decision. He looked out at the people in the room, hesitated, then said he was going to talk about something he generally brought up after the break: financing.

"That's right, you folks can do exactly the same as the biggest corporations in the country: borrow. Don't tell me why you can't get that kind of a loan," he said. "I'll tell you why you can. Because lending institutions are not in business to say no. But let's be realistic. You're not going to walk in off the street and have someone hand you the necessary capital. You have to go in there prepared. Here's how to do it.

"Imagine you've been out looking at properties for a couple of weeks, then you finally see something that you really like. Make an offer on it, a low offer. Of course it might take fifteen or twenty offers before you get a counter-offer but hey, no one said this wasn't work. When you do get a counter-offer," Glen paused, "negotiate. Remember, you're looking for a motivated seller, and those folks are out there, believe me. At some point you and a seller are going to settle on a price. Now you need your earnest money. Even if you don't have your loan, write out a check. That's right, but be sure and include the magic words *Contingent Upon. This check is contingent upon termite inspection. This check is contingent upon satisfactory completion of inspection for structural integrity.* What that means is, the check can't be deposited right away. Ladies and gentlemen, you've now bought yourself some time, it hasn't cost you a penny and now you've got this bargain-priced property to take to your banker. That," he said, "is how you get yourself a loan."

Glen scanned the room and smiled in satisfaction. "The next thing to ask is, are there problems with rental properties? You better believe it. You bet. No matter what you do you'll get your share of deadbeats and every once in a while you'll end up with a tenant who likes to kick holes in the walls. That comes with the territory, but I don't think you folks came here today because you're afraid of problems. As a matter of fact," Glen said, "if I was to ask what brought you here today a whole lot of you would probably say you're here because it's free. But you know what, I don't believe that's it. Basically you folks are self-starters and you came here today looking for that little extra bit of motivation that you feel you need to set your life on a somewhat new course. I think you're here to get motivated. After all, let's be honest, you know and I know that I can't teach you everything you need to know about real estate in one Saturday afternoon two-hour seminar, which is the reason I'm going to be making the material on the table right behind me available for your inspection during the break."

The people sitting nearest to Raleigh began to stir.

"The whole package," Glen said, "Doug's three best-selling books, a one-year subscription to Doug's magazine, *Success Unlimited*, and the eight forty-minute tapes usually go for $300, but as a special inducement I've been authorized to offer it to you for only $99.95."

Now he moved to wind things up. This low price was Doug's way of getting the word spread, Glen said, and then he closed by saying he'd answer any questions anyone might have during the break.

The only question Raleigh had was how to get out of there without drawing attention to himself. People were going directly up to Glen; others spread out around the table. He ran his fingers through his hair on the way to the door and immediately placed the peculiar smell that clung to his hands as coming from the liquid soap he'd washed with in the men's room, which some people in the corridor were heading toward. He lagged behind then hurried down two flights of stairs and caught an empty elevator on the ninth floor. On the eighth floor a crowd from King's got on. Still he couldn't relax and he knew why. Because against his better judgment he felt there might be something to what Glen had just said.

By God, the reason he'd come here today might not have had a thing in the world to do with making money. What an eye-opener.

The people who were here came to have someone light a fire under them. He saw why he'd been resisting everything. Because that wasn't how it was with him; it was just the opposite with him and then it hit: he'd come here looking to keep things as they were; hell, he liked his life, which was a fact he'd been overlooking just because he didn't like the way it had been going lately but he had no one but himself to blame for that, for letting things get out of hand, for thinking life was closing in when he'd simply gone a little stale, which could happen to anyone and surely that would pass of its own accord.

Not of its own accord. He had to get his damn attitude squared away. Old Glen laid it out: how you looked at things mattered.

Raleigh cut through the lobby. People were coming in off the street with wet clothes on. Son of a bitch, they hadn't been predicting rain. Standing near the door, he watched rain bounce off the pavement then decided to give Donna a call and warn her he was coming.

But she didn't respond as he thought she would. Instead of asking why he was coming home now, this early, which was what Raleigh wanted, she said, "We must be on the same wavelength."

"Oh?" Raleigh said.

"I was hoping you'd call. Do you remember Bill Oakley?"

Raleigh drew a blank.

"From the navy," Donna said.

"Oakley. Christ, you mean Annie? Yeah, I remember him."

"Well he called up right after you left."

It was the timing that tempered Raleigh's enthusiasm. This was a distraction. "What did he have to say?"

"It sounded like he just wanted to talk."

Raleigh had no idea when they'd last laid eyes on each other. "That's really something."

"I told you you'd be surprised. He was really disappointed that you weren't in. I guess he's driving out to California and he called during a pit stop from somewhere in Ohio."

She paused but he didn't take advantage of it.

"He'll be going right by here sometime later on so I told him to stop off, but he wasn't sure if he could take the time for that or not." She paused again and Raleigh knew that his silence was making her impatient. "Well, was that all right?"

"I guess so. Like you say, I'm surprised, that's all."

"I thought you'd be happy. He's your friend, not mine. Why are you so negative about everything lately?"

"I didn't know I was," he said. He didn't want to get into a hassle with Donna and spoil everything. "The whole thing sounds kind of goofy to me, that's all." He paused before he went on. "Did you see I took the letter and mailed it off to Scott?"

"Oh, good. Anyway," she said, "I asked Chick over for coffee and dessert later on. He was feeling pretty low this morning. Do you think you could stop at the liquor store? Get whatever we need to drink and you might as well pick up something for us to snack on."

"No problem."

"How did the seminar go?"

"Oh, about the way I figured," Raleigh said. "It was kind of silly. The speaker tried to rip us off with a bunch of expensive books and stuff. Listen, how are you feeling?"

She paused. "Me? I feel fine. Why?"

"You think you might feel like fooling around when I get home?"

It took a moment for her to answer. "Well, if that's what you have on your mind we've got a little problem."

"Don't tell me. Larry's home."

"How did you guess?"

"Damn. It's going to take a derrick to get that kid out of the house."

"Maybe we should wait until tonight."

"Sure. And about the time Chick leaves Oakley'll show up. I say we do it this way. You ask Larry if he wants to go to the Metropolitan." That was the downtown theater that showed dirty movies.

"Raleigh," Donna said, "stop that."

"I'm serious. Tell him I'll pay his way in. He can go with one of his friends."

"You're awful."

"Why? I'll pay for both of them."

"Look," she said, "just come home. I'll see if I can't work something out."

"I'm on the way."

When Donna opened the door the smile on her face told Raleigh all he had to know.

"Guess what?" she said.

He shook his head. "You tell me."

Donna was wearing faded cutoffs and a tee-shirt with ALOHA across the front in spangles.

"Well, Tiny called up and now Larry's over there."

Driving home Raleigh had made up a very short list of things he intended to abide by. Most importantly, he had to get his attitude squared away; second, he was going to ease up on himself, back off, and try to relax.

"Things are working out," Raleigh said, "by God."

"They generally do if you give them half a chance."

"I can't argue with that."

He stepped back and put the sack with the twelve-pack on the small hall table then turned around and circled Donna's waist. She was still standing in the doorway. The rain had stopped. The sky had brightened and there was a fresh clean smell in the air. Raleigh raised his hand until it held Donna's breast. It seemed to him that Donna, who was five feet one, had never stopped looking cute, yet she could handle things, there was no doubt about that. Yesterday she'd taken it upon herself to write back to Scott, not that it would change the situation any but at least it put an end to the bickering that Scott's letter had led to.

"Let's close the door."

He kicked it shut then dropped his hand to her behind as they made their way down the hall.

"What brought all this on, anyway?" she asked.

"Oh, probably all that good talk about money."

In the kitchen, as Donna made room for the beer in the refrigerator, Raleigh thought of something.

"Hey," he said, "you know what? No wonder I feel this hole in my gut. I forgot to get lunch."

"Well, I hope you don't want to eat now," Donna said, "because I don't think we should dawdle."

"By golly, I'm not the one who's dawdling." Then Raleigh changed his tone completely. "Yeah, it sure would be something to sit around and shoot the shit with old Annie again."

Donna smiled at that. Raleigh said he might as well go ahead and get ready, and a few minutes later, as he filed his nails in the bathroom at the top of the stairs, he heard her stop outside the door.

"Raleigh?"

"What?"

"I forgot to tell you something Oakley said."

"What's that?"

"His wife died."

Raleigh was aware of blinking several times, then his eyes opened wide. How in the world, he wondered, could anyone forget that? Raleigh tried to picture Oakley's wife but couldn't, and then he realized he'd never even known that Oakley had gotten married.

"Are you really saying," he said as he opened the door, "you forgot to tell me Annie's wife died?"

"Well," she said, "yes. I'm sorry. I would have told you if I'd remembered but that wasn't what he called about and I had other things on my mind you know. I can remember the exact words he used. He said he was calling to touch base. Look," Donna raised her voice as he got ready to interrupt, "are we really going to stand here and argue?"

That made Raleigh hesitate, then he said, "No" and added, "I'm not done," and went back into the bathroom.

Donna was sitting up in bed, smiling, with her top off, when he entered the bedroom. She had the top sheet doubled back so that it came to her waist. As he approached the bed he understood that she'd arranged herself for him, and that was disarming.

He approached slowly. Her smile seemed to play off the whiteness of both the top sheet and the pillow that was propped against the headboard and against which she was leaning. Along with a kind of playfulness Donna was radiating a whole lot of warmth.

Her arms went out.

"Come on," she said, "lie down slowpoke."

"I have to take my pants off first."

Instead, though, he leaned over, took the top sheet in his fingers, and without touching her at all pulled it down to the foot of the bed.

"There," he said.

One way or another, no matter which way they went, they'd end up making love exactly as they had a couple of thousand times before. He knew how things would go. Whenever Donna had this halfway dreamy look on her face it would be up to him to slow the pace down, which he could handle up to a point.

He stretched out beside her. Then they began to kiss, and as they made the moves they were each so familiar with, as they moved through it, it began to feel to Raleigh as if everything was right in place.

And as far as whatever it was that was working on him went, he'd lucked out in a way. He hadn't even been aware of anything until it was well underway. Regardless of anything else, there still were certain days that started out with the understanding that they'd make love sometime later on. To Raleigh that was like money in the bank. On a winter day that began with just that understanding—that they'd make love sometime later on—he found himself wondering why the fact that they wouldn't do anything they hadn't done countless times before never put a damper on it. Then that night as they were making love a thought came to him that immediately slipped away. Afterward he remembered what it was. The thing that might be different about their lovemaking, he thought, wasn't the lovemaking itself but him or them. That was it. Hell, he didn't think another thing about it but he felt somewhat disturbed, as if he hadn't come up with what he'd really been thinking. Yet he knew that he had. And over time this feeling of disturbance returned again and again. Even when it surfaced as a thought, as it sometimes did, it still wasn't there for him, but it was always at his heels, and it was always up ahead. And now, after months of getting worse, thanks to the seminar things seemed to have changed for the better.

Raleigh was dreaming. Donna was curled up on her side, her back against his. Then they were making love again. Then he heard Larry come in but Donna wouldn't stop. Larry was coming up the stairs; Raleigh knew that if he'd say something Donna would just tell him to stop being such a crab. The boy was in the hall, he was outside the door, which was opening and Larry was just about to catch them when Raleigh pulled out of the dream. Awake, breathless, with his head lifting off the pillow, he knew exactly where he was: in bed, and Donna was beside him with her eyes open.

"Did you just hear Larry come in?"

"No."

"You didn't?"

"No. And you didn't either because you were asleep. You were snoring."

"I thought I heard something," Raleigh said. "That's what woke me."

She didn't even answer that.

He lay back and under the strain of their silence a certain picture of Donna that he didn't much care for came to mind. She was staring vacantly ahead, as she'd sometimes do when they were at the table drinking coffee, as he'd seen her do when he thought she was paying attention to some TV program. Her short hair was parted on one side and held back by a barrette on the other. There were little pouches of flesh at either side of her mouth, and at the very bottom of her face her skin was starting to sag. Somehow that gave her face a square shape that it had never had before.

Neither one moved until, sometime later, Donna drew herself up and said, "I guess I better put some clothes on. Larry might walk in anytime."

Raleigh made a move as if to get off the bed on the other side. "Maybe I'll go ahead and take a shower," he said, but then he lay there thinking.

Several hours later, having fully emerged from the gray, dulled state he'd gradually slipped into, Raleigh, in an unthinking moment, blurted out some foolishness. He apologized, claimed he'd had too much to drink, and said he better get himself to bed.

This happened in the middle of the evening at a time when he could not have been more awake. Life was all around him, everywhere he turned: Larry, Donna; Lord, he wondered, how could he ever be removed from it.

But only hours earlier, after he'd gotten up and taken his shower, when he was down in his basement office, he hadn't been good for much of anything. He sat in the office quietly, without thinking. Sneezing snapped him out of it one time but only for a minute—just long enough to see that he was looking at a brass horse with green felt padding glued onto the base. Originally the horse had been intended as a paperweight, but now it sat on a shelf next to a heavy cardboard file. Then Donna had to call him twice before he went upstairs for dinner.

They were seated at the table eating grapefruit halves in silence when it registered on Raleigh that he was being uncommunicative and taking a kind of perverse satisfaction in that.

And Larry wasn't home yet either.

"I wonder where he is?" Donna said.

Raleigh shrugged. "He could be anywhere," he said, then thinking he should be more responsive, added, "Hell, he'll be along. No sense worrying."

Donna didn't react unless the way in which she kept on being her usual self was a reaction. She jumped up a couple of times to bring things out to the table that she'd forgotten. Once it was the jam and once a dish of black olives, as if that was what was missing, and Raleigh understood that she was going to let just about anything pass in order to keep things from becoming more difficult. After all, company was coming, company could show up anytime.

Larry walked in just as the dishes were being cleared. He stopped at the edge of the dining room then took out the red bandanna he was using for a handkerchief and blew his nose. He didn't have a whole lot to say for himself when he did speak, just that he hadn't expected he'd be gone this long and now he was running kind of late.

"Were you at Tiny's all this time?" Donna asked.

"Yes."

Raleigh couldn't think of any good follow-up to Donna's question.

"Well, if you're going to need the bathroom before you go to work," Donna said, "would you use it right away? I want to take a shower soon."

"Sure." Larry headed for his room.

Raleigh stayed clear of Donna as she rushed through the dishes. In almost no time Larry called, "Okay. I'm out. The bathroom's all yours."

Once Donna was upstairs Raleigh established himself in the kitchen. First he ran the trash out. Then he wiped the counter down. The two-inch-thick butcher-block top was so crisscrossed with knife cuts it now seemed dark and weathered. When was it, Raleigh tried to remember, that Scott had helped him tear the old counter out and put this one in? That must have been when Scott's ship was in the yards, Raleigh thought, right before the shakedown cruise to Gitmo. It seemed like Scott had been accumulating leave ever since then. You could carry up to sixty days on the books, he thought, then get paid for it when you were discharged or if you shipped over.

"Excuse me."

Raleigh was standing at the counter mindlessly brushing his fingertips over its roughened surface when Larry squeezed by. At the refrigerator he poured himself a glass of milk.

Again Raleigh couldn't think of what to say. He'd taken several bottles out of the cupboard and lined them up on the counter; the styrofoam ice bucket was on the counter too. Finally he poured himself a shot of Jim Beam.

"You missed a pretty good meal," Raleigh said.

"Yeah, well, I'll get something at work. You're getting a little head start on the evening, aren't you?"

"Hell, this settles my stomach. I ate too much."

"Right, Dad. Hey, Mom said one of your old navy buddies might stop by."

"I'll believe it when I see him come walking in that door."

"It would be nice though, wouldn't it?" Larry said. "Give you a chance to relive old times."

"What are you up to tonight?"

"There's a party out in the country at a farmhouse one of Tiny's friends is renting. I'm taking Cheryl after I get off work."

"You going to have her home at a decent hour?"

"Hope not. We probably won't even start to play until around eleven. Roy Craig's coming in so I can take off work early."

It wasn't really movement that caught Raleigh's eye, just the feeling that something was wrong, out of place. Then he saw Donna at the entrance to the kitchen and for some crazy reason he felt as if he'd been caught doing something wrong.

Raleigh gave her a dark, angry look. "I thought you were supposed to be washing up."

She was clearly taken back.

"Well," Larry said, "time for me to go to work."

"I wanted to call Harold before I forgot," Donna said. "It's Ina's birthday next week and I never know what to get her. Anyway, Harold would like you to call him when you get a chance." Then she added, "It's nothing important. It'll wait until tomorrow."

Larry squeezed past then touched Donna on the shoulder and said he'd see her later.

"I guess I'll go make myself look beautiful." Donna hesitated when Raleigh didn't answer then waited another second, and when he still didn't answer she turned and went upstairs.

Raleigh took a beer from the refrigerator. Then he took the seashell off the windowsill above the sink, but he put it right back down and started walking through the house, going from room to room. Finally, back in the kitchen, he looked out at the backyard, at the railroad ties that bordered Donna's flower garden. He could feel himself about to sink right back into it again when it occurred to him to go out to the utility room.

He did and there it was right across from the freezer, sitting on the table underneath the horseshoe: the aluminum martin house. He removed the sheet of clear plastic that he'd draped over it and promised himself that, by God, come hell or high water, it was going up first thing tomorrow: no need to get bit up by mosquitoes all damn summer long.

Raleigh finally quit fiddling with the TV and left on the *Saturday Night Movie*, which was just starting. But when Donna came down and asked him what he was watching Raleigh couldn't answer her.

"I guess I wasn't paying that much attention."

Donna frowned then moved directly in front of him. He was sitting in the recliner.

"Okay," she said, "what's wrong?"

Self-pity came to mind, but then Raleigh couldn't go along with that because self-pity made him think of someone who sat around feeling sorry for himself all the time and he didn't think that that was true of him. Hell, he didn't know. Finally, almost helplessly, he looked up at Donna and said, "It's just been that kind of a day."

Her eyes fixed on him. "Are you sure that's all this is?"

Raleigh saw there wasn't any anger, just concern. And instead of saying Yes, he was sure, he shrugged in a way that suggested the futility of it all, then looked over at the bowl of wax fruit on the mantel.

Donna snapped the TV off. "Maybe," she said, speaking slowly, "I should call up Chick and tell him not to come over."

Before Raleigh could answer the doorbell rang. At first neither one of them did anything, then Donna said, "That might be your friend."

Raleigh put his hands on the arms of the recliner, as if to raise himself.

"Are you going to answer it?"

He nodded yes, he was.

But he didn't mean it. He was bluffing. Standing, he expected Donna to stop him before he left the room, but she didn't and when he reached the hall he saw that it was Chick.

"Hi. Am I early?"

Raleigh shook his head. Relief, intense and unmistakable, washed over him. It wasn't Oakley. "No, you're right on time. *Donna*, Chick's here," Raleigh yelled. "Come on in."

His neighbor was wearing a nautical blazer and banana-colored pants.

"It's starting to look like my buddy won't make it," Raleigh said. "Did Donna tell you about him?"

"Only that an old friend of yours called and said he might be stopping off."

"Chances are I wouldn't even recognize him anymore."

"Oh, sure you would."

"I probably wouldn't know him if he came right up and tapped me on the shoulder."

"Hi, Chick," Donna said as they walked into the wood-paneled rec room. Raleigh noticed Donna sneak a worried look at him.

"Evening. I was about to tell Raleigh, this fellow might surprise you and show up yet."

Chick and Donna started talking right away. The length of polished wood mounted on the wall above the mantel reminded Chick of Hilton Head, he said, though actually Donna had brought it home from Wharfside, the store where she worked, where they sold just about everything: wicker furniture, straw hats, Chinese fans, driftwood, and a lot of foreign-type clothing. Sometimes he'd stop at the Mister Donut right across from Wharfside, Chick said, as he angled for the taco chips and dip.

"Why don't you see if Chick's ready for something to drink."

"What can I get you?"

"I believe I'll hold off for a little while." Chick turned to Donna. "Barbara would have really enjoyed getting together like this."

"Then we'll do it again when she gets back." Donna seemed to be considering something. "Larry said he's coming back here after work to pick up Cheryl. Well, she's certainly welcome to come over here and wait with us."

Chick waved his hand in a listless way, as if he was pushing that idea aside. "You know, you hate to complain about your own kid, but I don't know. . . ."

Raleigh perked up. "Cheryl giving you a hard time, is she?"

"I guess you heard me say she quit school. Well, what really disappointed me was the way she went about it. I don't know. It just seems to me that kids are pretty thoughtless sometimes. Maybe irresponsible's the right word."

"Doggone it, move over buddy. If that's the way you feel you've got yourself some company."

Chick laughed. "Maybe I'll take you up on that drink after all."

In the kitchen Raleigh suddenly realized he was feeling pretty good. Scotch on the rocks, Seven and Seven, and he'd stick with Jim Beam. At least he didn't feel as low as he had before.

"Here you go," he said to Donna, then to Chick. Then Chick picked up on some point he'd been making.

"I'll say this. Larry's the only good thing to come out of this whole mess. Ever since Cheryl turned sixteen she's been saying boys her own age bore her. I'm glad to see that's changing."

"I told him," Raleigh said, "you be sure to have that girl home at a decent hour."

The conversation jumped to Scott who, it was explained, was going to stay in the navy for another year.

"He'll probably make a career of it," Raleigh said. "I'd just like to see him get his education first, you know, then decide what he wants to do. Of course, if he's got his mind made up, why that's it."

"You suppose things ever get any easier?" Chick asked.

"You'd think it would ease up some when they get older, but I don't see it."

A kind of knowing laughter followed. Time moved right along despite a certain undercurrent in the room which Raleigh was determined not to let get the better of him. Donna wasn't out to spoil his time, he knew, but how was he supposed to enjoy himself when she kept sneaking those quick, apprehensive looks at him. Nor could he ignore the sweetness that he tasted whenever he drank bourbon without ice for any period of time. To cut it Raleigh went out to the kitchen for a beer. Coming back he stopped in front of his neighbor.

"There's something I've been meaning to ask you," he said. "I don't know a damn thing about the stock market."

"Yeah," Donna said. "Any hot tips?"

"No," Raleigh said, "I'm serious. I've got an expert here, I might as well take advantage of it."

"Maybe Chick likes to leave his work at the office," Donna said.

Chick said no. "Just let me give Cheryl a call before I get started, then we'll see if I can't make some money for you."

Raleigh directed him to the phone at the foot of the stairs. Then he said to Donna, "Do you know there's a spot on your blouse?"

"Oh no," Donna said, looking down, "how did that happen?"

She left for the kitchen and almost immediately Raleigh felt uneasy, as if something could happen but before he could take it any further than that Donna returned carrying a tray with a cheeseball, crackers, and a knife, which she set on the coffee table.

"How's that?"

"Better," Raleigh nodded. "A lot better." Then he said, "If Oakley's not here by now I'm pretty sure he won't be coming."

"You could be right."

"But I wish I knew what that call was about. I bet I haven't seen him in twenty years, maybe more than that."

"I thought we decided he called for old time's sake."

"Shit," Raleigh said. "Maybe you decided that. I didn't."

"So what are you saying," Donna said, "that you don't want him to stop by? Because that's what it sounds like."

"No. I'm saying it's getting kind of late. Are you sure you told me everything he said."

"Look, don't start blaming me because you weren't home. If you hadn't gone to that damn seminar then maybe you would have been here and you could have talked to him yourself."

Raleigh didn't answer. Then Chick came back and for a second Donna put her hand on the breast pocket of the pearl gray blouse, right where the spot had been. Then she pointed over at the cheeseball.

"I'm not going to pass this around," she said; "you two can just help yourselves."

Chick nodded. "I hear you were going to that deal at the Penfield Inn," he said to Raleigh.

"That's right. I noticed I didn't see you over there."

"I was on the phone talking to my customers most of the afternoon. What was it, one of those inspirational sessions?"

"Motivation, inspiration, you name it."

"Raleigh knew it would be a rip-off before he ever went," Donna said.

"But I don't feel like I wasted my time."

"Going there shows you were looking to your future. A guy would be foolish if he didn't," Chick said.

"This doggone speaker they had was slicker than a whistle," Raleigh said, "but about all he ever came up with was a bunch of real estate schemes. You have any opinion on that?"

"Be cautious. That's my eleventh commandment. I tell people who ask me about the stock market, Not everybody belongs in the market, but I'll say this, if you went to that deal this afternoon then you're probably about ready to invest."

Raleigh nodded.

"Then the first thing you want to think about is"—and now Chick looked from Raleigh to Donna—"what are your objectives? Do you know?" When neither one said anything he said, "After you get that clear in your own mind, then nothing anyone's ever going to tell you about the stock market is more important that this: it's your money that's on the line so you're the ones who have to take responsibility for your investments."

Raleigh nodded. "I go along with that."

"I'll give you an example of that. And this really happens. A customer will call me up and say, Chick, I've got a little extra money, what looks good? Hey," Chick said, "I'm not going to turn down a commission."

What are your objectives? That was reverberating in Raleigh's mind. Son of a bitch. He didn't know if he'd been preparing for this or battling against it. What are your objectives? A sense of panic crept in. He looked around and when he saw Chick he couldn't remember who

Chick was, not until he heard what Chick was saying and then the panic vanished.

"I'll get him the best information I can," Chick said, "but I'd have to give the same information to the next customer that called too, right? Now from the customer's standpoint you know there's got to be a better way to do it. Instead of asking your broker, What looks good, you should do your homework first. Be ready to put some time into this."

Raleigh nodded. "No problem. Like you say, it's my money."

"Unless you want to go with something like a mutual fund where you'd have professionals handling your money for you, which isn't a bad way to go."

"I kind of like the idea of doing it myself."

"Then there's one basic rule you as a small investor absolutely want to follow: always do an analysis of any company you think you want to buy."

"We wouldn't know how to go about it," Donna said.

"It sounds like a lot but there's not that much to learn," Chick said.

"We should be writing this down," Donna said.

"If a company's still interesting after you check it out, *that's* when you call your broker to see if he knows something you don't. If he doesn't then you can tell him to execute the transaction and he ought to keep you from being out-timed."

Raleigh nodded. This sounded like a long-term approach. He could respond to that. He could learn. He could subscribe to those magazines Chick was mentioning and he could read the *Wall Street Journal* too. This was what he wanted to hear. Then Chick was waiting, looking at him, and he saw it was his turn to say something.

"You're sure giving me a lot to think about," Raleigh said.

Chick smiled. "That's the whole idea."

The doorbell rang and everything that Chick had said was wiped away.

"Probably Cheryl. I took you up on your offer and asked her to come over," Chick said.

Raleigh went to the door to let her in.

"Hi. Is Dad here?"

After Raleigh said yes he couldn't contain himself. He couldn't keep from stepping onto the porch and looking up and down the street to see if anyone was coming.

"It's going to be bright out in the country tonight," Raleigh said.

"I thought it would save time if I waited for Larry over here."

What a get-up, Raleigh thought. She had oversized owlish-looking horn-rimmed glasses on, for one thing, and her hair was pulled back in a schoolteacher's bun. No makeup on either, and the clothes were just as crazy. She was wearing a man's suit jacket that was big enough for someone else to get in there with her, and then she had a man's white shirt on and a skinny black tie. It was more like a costume than anything, Raleigh thought, taking one long final look up and down the street before they started in.

"I was just listening to a tape of Larry's band," she said. "God, they're really good. It's just insane that they're stuck here in Penfield."

"What's insane?" Chick asked as they entered the rec room.

"That this is a weekend night and Larry's band doesn't even have a gig. Hi, Donna."

"Hi. What a pretty bag."

It was cloth with a plaid design and wooden handles.

Raleigh fought off the impulse to say out loud what he'd been thinking, that maybe Oakley really wasn't coming.

"It kind of looks like the Flessner family's barging in on you," Chick said.

"Yeah. I hope my coming over doesn't bum you out."

"Glad to have you," Raleigh said. "Come over anytime."

"I don't know about that pal of yours," Chick said. "Seems to me like he's got you hanging fire."

"I've about given up on him."

After the situation was explained to Cheryl she had a suggestion. "You could call up Holiday Inn and see if your friend checked in. Most of the motels only hold reservations until six o'clock."

"The hell with it," Raleigh said. "Help yourself to the cheese."

Donna said, "Your dad was just giving us some free advice."

Chick downplayed that but said he had just a couple more things he wanted to say, then he'd be quiet.

"No. Go on. This is really a help." Donna turned to Raleigh. "It's crazy of us not to be writing this down."

"Well," Chick said, "if you do invest use a method. That's important. Be consistent. Some of my customers only buy blue-chip stocks, then I have others who won't buy anything but industry leaders. Oh," Chick said, "in airlines you're talking Delta, in railroads Burlington Northern or Union Pacific, in drugs Merck, that type thing.

"I'll tell you what the pros do. They pick the best industry, then they'll buy four or five stocks in that one industry."

"It'll take us a while to get the hang of this," Donna said. She quickly turned to Cheryl. "Now that you're back do you know what you're going to do? Jobs are kind of scarce right now."

"I heard they're looking for instructors at Slimnastics so maybe I'll apply over there."

Chick asked directions to the bathroom, then Donna went to put the coffee up, leaving Raleigh all alone with Cheryl. Dressing the way she did was like wearing a damn flag; he thought of the plain-looking gal in the porno films who takes off her glasses, let's down her hair, and then goes hog wild. Just can't get enough of it, Raleigh thought, but then he started talking about martins, how they'll come back every year if you get them to nest just once.

"Of course, sometimes they'll surprise you," he said, "and have two broods the same summer. But you can count on one thing, they'll be gone by the second week in August. That's just the way they are," he said, then Chick came back and Raleigh saw he was excited.

"You know what I thought of?" Chick asked without sitting down. Raleigh said he didn't. "The cemetery stocks. You'll appreciate that because of your interest in real estate, which is the one asset all cemeteries have: their land. There's your hedge against inflation, but on the other hand cemetery customers pay in today's dollars for tomorrow's services. That could make for a very interesting play."

"Now who died?" Donna asked with a smile as she came back in.

Then the door slammed and Larry called, "Hello." The next second he was in the room with them.

"You're here," he said when he saw Cheryl. "Great. Howdy, everybody."

All of a sudden everything seemed to have speeded up.

Seely Haskell wanted to work, Larry said, so he got off even earlier than he expected.

"You must have some money rat-holed away we don't know about," Donna said.

"No. I just don't spend that much," Larry said. He turned to Cheryl. "They're jamming over at Buddy Davenport's."

"Really? What about the party?"

"Change in plans," he said, and he went running up the stairs for his guitar.

Cheryl stood as if in anticipation of leaving.

Chick said something about being young again. Then he said, "I think it would be kind of nice to get a camper and do like your buddy's doing and drive out west."

"I guess Oakley's going through a real hard time," Raleigh said. Chick appeared surprised. "Oh," Raleigh said, "didn't Donna tell you either? His wife died."

"Damn it, Raleigh, will you get off my back," Donna said. "Am I supposed to be responsible for every single thing people I've never even met tell me?"

"No," Raleigh said, "but it seems like you wouldn't forget something like that."

Donna didn't answer right away. Instead of answering she glared at him. Raleigh responded with a steady stare of his own.

"Well, I guess we're getting to that age," Chick said, "and don't anyone ask what age because if you have to ask you haven't reached it yet."

No one paid him any mind.

"I'd appreciate it if you'd clear something up for me," Donna said.

Raleigh's stare didn't waver. He wasn't backing down this time, by God, just the opposite. Whatever it was that had been building was finally coming to a head.

"You don't want Oakley stopping here, do you?" Donna said. "That's been obvious from the first time I mentioned his name." Raleigh's eyes remained on hers. "What I want to know is, why not?"

Then Larry came back holding his guitar case. He was wearing a black tee-shirt and a red vest.

"I'll tell you why," Raleigh said. He never even thought to deny it. "Because I don't like him."

For a moment everything hung, then Raleigh realized he was furious, enraged, he was madder than a wet hen. He wanted to go on and repeat what he'd just said, shout it out at the top of his lungs, but even as he glared at Donna her eyes were growing wider and the momentum that had taken him this far started to slip away. He could feel it. It faded as the anger in Donna's eyes turned to disbelief.

"I can't believe you just said that."

"Why not?" Raleigh said, but Jesus Christ he'd blown it. He knew it.

Larry was trying hard, he saw, to keep from laughing.

"If I tell you I don't like someone," Raleigh said, "I think you should believe me."

"But Dad, you're the one who said he was your buddy," Larry said, and that was it. That did it.

That really set them off. Raleigh knew without question that from here on anything he'd say would make it worse, would only make it funnier to them. He could not believe it. After coming this far something still was missing and now there wasn't a damn thing he could do about it.

Then he himself started to laugh. It was some impulse within him that he couldn't control. Keep hold of yourself, he thought. Cheryl and Chick looked at him as if he was crazy but that was all right. Laughing didn't automatically mean something's funny or that you're happy. It could also mean you felt the way he did. He hoped they had sense enough to know Donna and Larry weren't out to put him down. After all, he'd been an evil-tempered son of a bitch all day long and they'd been putting up with that.

"Dad," Larry said as he forced himself to quit laughing, "sometimes you're too much." He turned to Cheryl. "Come on. We better get going."

Of course, he knew that it was dumb to wish they'd stick around; they wanted to start their evening. It was just that there was a sudden surge of feeling for his son, for his family.

Standing next to his recliner Raleigh kept his hands at his side as Chick and Donna said some final words to Cheryl and Larry. Then he slowly raised them, ground the meaty, hardened heel of one hand into the upturned palm and heel of the other. By God, he'd send them off as if things couldn't be better. He checked his watch. It was the middle of the evening.

Raleigh could see himself moving between Cheryl and Larry, putting an arm around each one's shoulder. That would be the way to do it he thought, and he started for them then reconsidered and veered toward Donna, who quit talking. He'd stand with her and wave good-bye.

She stepped back when he was about a step away. He put his arm on her shoulder anyway but she kept her distance, which made him feel awkward.

She seemed puzzled, uncertain of him. That's the road to negative thinking, Raleigh thought. It seemed to him as if having his arm across her shoulder was something Donna felt she had to tolerate; Raleigh looked away, toward Larry, then he turned back to Donna and smiled.

"I know what we could do. Let's have another kid. Maybe that would solve our problem."

Raleigh saw she didn't appreciate that. Not a hint of a smile anywhere, which figured.

"What problem?" Donna asked.

It was supposed to be a joke, he wanted to say, a goofy remark. And she knew it. Maybe she didn't. Anymore it seemed like he couldn't get anything right. As Raleigh thought that, a long-sought answer simply presented itself. He was going to die.

By God, he was going to die.

That's all there was to it. Not that that was something he hadn't always known, he thought, but there it was. That was the thought he'd been after, by God, that was the thought that was after him. Everything started to swirl except for one thing. He couldn't just stand there, he had to say something, but it was as if Donna had stepped too far back and he couldn't see her. Still, I'm not shaking in my boots, he thought, and he didn't feel abandoned either. Without it reflecting his feelings a grin broke out.

"Sorry," he said. "That must have been the booze talking. I spoke out of turn."

"No you didn't," Larry said when Donna didn't answer.

"It's time for me to get to bed."

"What's wrong with Dad?" Larry asked as Raleigh made his way out of the room but, as if she'd lost her tongue, Donna wasn't answering.

On the stairs Raleigh knew he'd never been less tired in his life. To call it pathetic almost missed the point: it almost seemed like punishment, he thought. The one thing he couldn't keep out of his mind was the same thing he'd been afraid to think about: he was going to die. How had he ever come up with something like that he wondered as the bathroom door closed behind him. The bathroom was the only room upstairs that he could lock.

He sat without moving on the edge of the tub, then thought, Piss on it, and took off his shoes, stripped off his socks. This was a heck of a thing to be doing with a roomful of people downstairs.

When his clothes lay in a pile on the floor he stepped into the shower, turned on the water, then tested it with his hand.

Too hot. After making adjustments he leaned forward and bowed his head, wetting his hair. Then he backed up, cupped his hands, and caught some water, which he threw on himself.

This was the way he always did it.

Raleigh was still under the shower when the water lost its heat, became cold. Chilled, he turned the water off but then heard himself being called and turned it right back on.

Then off, quickly, on, like a child flicking a light switch, until he realized that was Annie calling. Man oh man, he thought, reaching for a towel. He walked to the window where he parted the curtain.

Yes sir, by God, there he was. He was standing next to the LTD that was parked under the street light in front of his house. And even if Oakley's hair had still been dark and even if he'd still been skinny, not half bald with a good sized gut, he couldn't have looked anymore like himself. There were some people you just recognize, Raleigh thought, and there was no mistaking him.

"Yo, Raleigh," Oakley called. He waved and motioned with his hand. "Come on down, pal. Chagaoo." And then he shouted, "Hey, did you think I wasn't coming?"

Raleigh smiled and shook his head. Still, in a way he could hardly believe it. Except it had been like this all damn day long, one thing after another, without let-up. This was just more of the same, Raleigh thought as he closed the curtain, then put on his pants and unlocked the bathroom door.

Blackburn

Blackburn heard on the network news that six inches of rain had fallen in less than an hour in Galveston, Texas, yesterday. Four people were known dead, seven more were unaccounted for, and there had been millions of dollars in property damage to the downtown business area.

Galveston. That was where the boy lived now. Blackburn wondered if he should try to get in touch. Frances and the boy, Kevin, wrote and spoke to each other often; surely if anything were wrong, he thought, Frances would make it her business to notify him. Still, he wanted to assure himself—he wanted to know for an absolute fact—that everything was all right.

He'd call, he decided, later, sometime this evening. He'd call Frances rather than the boy and take the opportunity to check one final time and make absolutely sure she had the flight number and his arrival time.

He'd been away far too long.

Not that Blackburn believed there was any such thing as a fresh start. He wouldn't delude himself. At some point, as Blackburn saw it, you simply come to realize that you're never getting out from under. No matter what I do, he'd say, I wake up everyday to a guaranteed defeat. That doesn't mean you kill yourself (you don't) or that you don't keep plugging. It meant, in Blackburn's case, that he didn't have to spend time tracking down the source of his fatigue. He understood why he was so sleepy all the time.

Now Blackburn recalled Frances in her sleeveless yellow dress, the one that came to her knees and was rather low-cut. Since her figure then, as now, surely was, by most standards anyway, just in proportion, it was somewhat surprising that clothes had never looked particularly smart on her. Curiously though, there had been something about that that he'd found appealing.

He thought it had to do with the unassuming way in which she conducted herself, which perhaps explained, at least to some extent, why Frances, unlike so many other people, hadn't responded with wisecracks or sarcasm when he, in unguarded or characteristic moments, had wondered out loud about abstract things like reality or outer space or even where the world was headed.

In any event, that was a reasonable description of his wife, he thought, and of her yellow dress, which he could remember her taking off after they'd returned from seeing some movie or other, after he'd taken the babysitter home.

They were in their bedroom; it was sometime after midnight.

He came up behind her, stood very close.

"What's that that I feel?" she said laughing, looking back over her shoulder.

"What do you think?"

It wasn't for arbitrary or obscure reasons that that scene came to mind.

Indeed. He couldn't imagine what kind of life he would have led had he not married Frances, which indicated to him that, despite impressive evidence to the contrary, he probably didn't know himself very well. Had he not married, he imagined he would have eaten in those places where the vegetables are steamed to death, where jello salad topped with shredded carrot is a staple, where there's a special of the day everyday and once a week it's swiss steak.

So what if his life was not a shining example. It's not really a matter of how your life ultimately turns out, he consoled himself. Looking at life that way reduced life to a problem that you had to get right, or so he told himself—this forty-eight-year-old man whose quarters in the Sheepshead Bay section of Brooklyn left much to be desired.

And why, since it wasn't his, had he put any effort at all into keeping that property up, or making improvements, doing lawn and garden work from spring to fall, for instance, gratis, and how many times had he taken a plane to a storm window that had warped or done some patchwork on the crumbling cement steps? True, he was better served by the premises because of that, yet that only masked his intentions. Though lately he'd been staying put, there was a rootless coloration to his life that he very much disliked, and working on the place fulfilled a need he had to belong, to feel he wasn't transient.

It created that illusion, anyway, and if he could squeeze some mileage out of an illusion he would do so. Not surprisingly, when Blackburn tried reaching Frances she wasn't in. It was, after all, the Declaration Day weekend. Perhaps she'd gone to her sister's house. He tried the boy, let the phone ring and ring, and when he hung up was surprised by the relief he felt just in knowing the phone in Kevin's apartment still worked.

He boarded the plane in a drizzle. The flight, as he expected it would be, was entirely uneventful. The plane touched down then taxied on a north-south runway that, as far as Blackburn could tell, hadn't existed when he'd last been in town. Even from a distance it was clear the one-story terminal had been extensively remodeled. Inside a bank of phones stood opposite the new baggage area. He dialed her number. The man who answered said no one by the name of Frances Blackburn lived there.

"Are you sure?"

The man was positive.

Damn it, Blackburn thought, I can feel that goddamn shit-eating grin of mine spreading all over my face. Why does this happen to me?

"Okay. Thanks."

There were some things about which it was best not to think, he told himself.

Outside an immensely overweight cabdriver wearing a Budweiser belt buckle said it would be five dollars for the fifteen-minute drive into town, to Carlyle's Downtown Motor Inn.

Though he'd told himself, Don't think, he knew that wasn't the easiest advice to follow. After all, wasn't he the one who would awaken suddenly with his heart racing as if urgent business had been pressing on his mind even while asleep? And to make matters worse, to complicate things, once he was awake, falling back asleep was out of the question.

The motel, which was at the top of a semi-circular drive, seemed inspired by the sort of colorful illustration sometimes found in a children's storybook. It billed itself as a convention center, offered banquet facilities, had a lobby with nooks and crannies, hanging plants, and a little waterfall.

"Can I help you?" the desk clerk asked.

He'd called from Carlyle Airport a few minutes ago, he explained, and now wanted to check in.

"Here you go, Mr. Blackburn," the desk clerk, wearing a snappy green blazer with the motel's logo on the breast pocket, said, pushing the registration form across the counter. She rattled on as he filled it out and in this way he learned that the Carlyle Lounge, located right off the lobby, was open until 2 A.M. nightly; happy hour was underway right now. He smiled at that.

Of course, common sense prevailed. First things first. Blackburn sought out room 307, turned on the air conditioner to get the stale air circulating, then showered, shaved, slipped into an open-neck floral shirt, tan slacks, and a pair of scruffy half boots that zipped to the ankle. Loose change that he'd earlier placed on the dresser he now put in his pocket. He snapped the TV off then checked the mirror. It was Blackburn's impression that people who labor under the burden of great personal sadness often come across to other people—the unwary—as other-worldly. He reserved judgment. Yet, oddly, news, whether national or international just so long as it fell within a certain range—anything from the disorderly, on the one hand, to the disastrous, on the other—he could accept without blinking, without reservation; that was his nature.

The Carlyle Lounge was very nearly full.

Though each of the four overhead fans revolved at a different speed, Blackburn felt supremely confident. The young man seated next to him, Ferris Bergstrom, was undoubtedly responsible for that. An assistant manager of the grain company in Arcola, a town some forty miles away, he kept turning on his stool and looking in a kind of anxious, overheated way at each woman who walked by. That was something Blackburn could relate to.

"You wouldn't believe the money I make," Bergstrom said shortly after striking up a conversation. It turned out he was only twenty-four and he generally came to the Carlyle Lounge once a week. "There's not much going on in Arcola."

"This seems like a lively place."

The lounge attracted a cross section: people ranged in age from early twenties to fifties and sixties; they dressed in everything from jeans to business suits, and a redheaded woman with hoop earrings had on a swanky midnight blue outfit. Blackburn's attention had been caught by a young woman in a purple vinyl raincoat who was now seated at the service end of the bar. She'd returned his smile on one of her several trips to the john, and because of that—with only that to go on—Blackburn had concluded she was available, she could be picked up. However, he was in no hurry.

"Yeah, I guess you'd have to say my future's pretty much guaranteed so long as I stay in Arcola," Ferris said. "The manager's sixty-two and when he retires I'm in line to take his place."

"Sounds good. Do you come from this area?" Blackburn asked.

But Ferris wasn't listening.

A blond bony woman with her right arm crooked at the elbow so that her forearm crossed her chest, protecting both her small breasts from any accidental contact, had squeezed between them, but she had no luck at all in getting the bartender's attention.

"Hey, Tommy," Ferris finally called.

That help notwithstanding the woman ignored him, and during the minute or so it took the bartender to make the two tequila sunrises that she'd ordered, Blackburn understood Ferris was wracking his brains trying to come up with something to say.

When she returned to her booth with the drinks Ferris, looking pained, could only shake his head. "The women in here sure are hard to get to know," he said.

"It runs in streaks. Your luck will change."

"I guess so."

Blackburn nodded, but suddenly he didn't feel quite so relaxed in his drinking. Soon afterward he rose from his stool and, drink in hand, walked toward the end of the bar. A stool next to the woman he'd had his eye on had just been vacated.

"Mind if I sit down?"

Perhaps fifteen minutes after joining her Blackburn determined to put an end to the small talk. "Look, I've got a room here." He said this in a way that allowed for no misinterpretation.

She eyed him coolly, hesitated, asked, "Are you married?"

"Right."

"I wasn't sure. By any chance do you have an arrangement with your wife?"

"No, I just cheat," Blackburn said.

Then absolutely uninvited a thought came to him. Kevin would not be thrilled by this. Far from it. Similarly, years earlier, though there had been no rational explanation for the shock he felt, he'd realized that this boy, who at the time had an unquestioning faith in him, would one day learn a very painful lesson at his expense. He'd been melancholy at the thought of that and at the thought of the confusion awaiting Kevin. He wondered how the girl was doing.

Bernadette, having removed a pink barrette from her hair as they walked down the corridor, was way ahead of him, but as anyone but Blackburn could see she felt constrained not to be overt about it, not, that is, until the door to room 307 had closed behind them.

Blackburn, immediately struck by how cold the room had gotten, wondered, as he crossed the room, if by becoming chilled some obscure sanitary purpose might not be served. He turned the air conditioning down.

"There," he said, "that's better." He turned to face her.

She'd removed her blouse; her breasts were smaller than he would have expected; the nipples were large and dark.

"Oh," he said, "Bernadette."

Then Blackburn went directly to the chair on which she'd hung the blouse and picked it up. He hoped this wouldn't make her peevish.

He held it out to her.

Perhaps decisiveness was not to be expected from someone who managed to proceed with his life only by making drastic substitutions. If Blackburn ever thought that way he no longer did.

Bernadette took the blouse from him and, holding it between her fingers, remaining motionless as possible, without quite managing to look disdainful, waited for an explanation.

"If you don't mind," Blackburn said, smiling tentatively, "here's what I'd like."

She waited.

"Do you think you'd be willing to go outside, then knock on the door, and when I answer could you pretend you're selling magazine subscriptions door to door?"

She looked up at the ceiling, rolled her eyes.

"You're trying to win a trip. That's your sales pitch. You need points."

"Then what?"

"I invite you in. Will you do that for me?"

"You're a funny one, you know that? You really are."

"See, you come in because even though I don't look like I'm really interested you want to try for the sale."

"Then what happens?"

"Nothing that we both won't enjoy."

Without a word she put the blouse back on then buttoned it up. Blackburn existed in a state of suspension. It was not until she reached for her leather handbag, which was also on the chair, that she let her eyes meet his, and only then did he see she wasn't taking off, only then did he see she was agreeing.

If Anyone is, then Whoever it is who's in charge knows what He's doing, Blackburn thought. Things were working out *that* well.

Bernadette was now rummaging through her handbag, and when she found what she was looking for she turned to him. "You want to do a number first?"

"Hell, yes."

Then Blackburn awoke to his responsibility. He woke with a start. Frances, Jesus. He had to see Frances. That was the whole point of his trip. How in God's name, Blackburn wondered, had he let himself get this distracted. The covers had been kicked to the foot of the bed; the bedspread lay on the floor.

He moved cautiously. It was dark in the room and, he saw from the window, dark outside. The bathroom was a goddamn mess.

As he stopped at the desk in the lobby to check on the time, he thought, This is really a fool's errand, but being on the street in the middle of the night was nothing new to him, was par for the course, was something he'd learned to turn to his advantage, at least in one respect: it gave him a way to define himself, but he derived very little benefit from that.

On more nights than he cared to remember he'd been awakened by something that, he said, could best be described as a feeling of overwhelming intensity. It couldn't be ignored or dismissed. He would get dressed. And after he'd been out walking for awhile, invariably at a furious pace, with questions hammering away at him, questions he couldn't find the words for, a shift would occur and it would be obvious the intensity had subsided, leaving him in large part drained, in need of something, something positive, something formulated, feasible, specific; a destination. There, just that: a destination. It suddenly became crucial that he know where he was going.

Down the driveway, turn left at the four-way stop. There was no justice. Everyone knew that. There was no injustice, either, which was another way of saying the same thing exactly, or so he believed; at least he thought he did. Averill's was gone, he saw; no surprise. It went back to the Patriarch Abraham. Even as a child that story had disturbed him. Abraham, who, whatever his misgivings, had built an altar and would have gone ahead and sacrificed his son. Here Warren Street turned hilly. Blackburn couldn't imagine doing that himself. Later on, much later, certain human accomplishments made quite an impression on him. Insanity, that plea. To think that you might not be guilty of something that you'd done because you weren't yourself when you did it: that idea must have required inspiration. It spoke well of Man that he could imagine that. An idea like that was worthy of religion, and if the idea was abused by certain people, that discredited the people, not the idea. Look at language. What could be more basic? Yet usage was often at odds with definition; the explanation was, Meanings changed, but still, what a peculiar system. The light was green, no traffic though, so he crossed to the even-numbered side of Warren Street and angled toward the Palmer Commercial Building. It was so easy for things to get out of whack. The first door he tried was locked; the next one opened.

A few moments later, as Blackburn stood in the lobby looking up at the directory, a man turned the corner of one of the two corridors that fed into the lobby and approached him. The man was clearly acting in some official capacity. He had on a green workshirt.

"Can I help you?"

"Hi," Blackburn said, "how you doing?"

"Not too bad."

For no apparent reason Blackburn seemed on the verge of ironic laughter. "I used to work for Lehman & Small," he said. "They still here on the third floor?"

"Sure are. Why don't you come back in the morning, okay?"

Blackburn hastily explained that he'd ducked into the building just so he could cut through it. Would that be all right?

The man barely nodded. Then he gave each one of the four doors that made up the main entrance a quick check, turned, and headed toward the corridor from which he'd come. Blackburn fell into step with him.

Someone departing the building late must have left a door ajar, the man said, otherwise Blackburn never would have gained admittance. After nine all the doors were locked.

"Is that something new?"

"Been that way as long as I've been working here."

As they were passing the elevators the man pointed to a chair, more precisely to a book on the chair. It looked like a ledger.

"That's the security log. Anyone comes or goes after nine, we ask those people to sign in and out."

"You want me to?"

"Nah," the man said. Then he walked Blackburn to the Montague Street exit and unlocked the door.

A gizmo on the First National Bank of Carlyle blinked the weather: thirty-six degrees. The wind had a bite to it.

As far as work went, he'd been siding houses, off and on, for quite some time, for Gould Enterprises. A hammer-and-truck operation, pure and simple. Joe Gould's garage served as the warehouse. He crossed Race Street. It was the kind of situation Blackburn liked.

It was eerily familiar now. Houses he was passing had toys scattered on the sidewalk and in the yards. Then he could see it. There it was, second from the corner: the box-shaped house with a steep roof they'd bought back when mortgages could be had for seven percent or less: six rooms, a weathered clapboard exterior, enclosed porch, dry basement—.

And the lights were on. He felt a bit breathless about this, stepped closer. In front. Then he was on the lawn, near the window, half hidden by the shrubbery: he was going to look inside.

What have I been thinking about, he thought. My God. Just what in the hell have I been thinking about? He turned away in amazement. Frances wasn't here; he knew that. Frances was in the hospital. How could he have forgotten a thing like that? She was in the new wing, in fact, in a room on the second floor.

"Frances," Blackburn said as he entered.

She was lying in bed, reading.

"Oh, it's you. They weren't supposed to let you in if you showed up. Dr. Farber left orders."

By the time he'd reached the hospital not only was it light outside but the light had gained a midday quality. Blackburn only barely recognized his wife. There was something blurred or indistinct about her now. In bed clothes, with her hair graying and somewhat unkempt, almost swallowed by the pillows that had been arranged behind her head, she seemed to blend or fade right in with the place. Blackburn felt uneasy. He knew she wasn't in the hospital to have a child, but as for why she was here, that was eluding him.

"What's wrong, Frances?"

Her response was limited: a shrug. It was a nonresponse. She seemed removed, even when she finally spoke.

"It's a female complaint."

"What's that mean?"

"It's vaginal, Marty."

He waited and finally she spoke again.

"There's inflammation of the torture chamber."

Blackburn wasn't sure he'd heard correctly. He thought that he might laugh. He was nonplussed. He took that as a criticism. He felt personally affronted. What a putdown. Two can play that game, he thought, and yet—.

And yet he knew that in some way he'd induced that response, in fact was as responsible for it as the dreamer was for the words spoken by all the people in his dream, which increased his uneasiness, made his uneasiness turn to outright apprehension.

There was cold comfort for Blackburn in thinking, You're being put to the test, cold comfort not because Blackburn believed there was no Tester—he wasn't sure of that, or even very interested—but because he felt there was no answer, and if that meant you had to make up your own answer (and it seemed to Blackburn it must), then his feeling was, What kind of flabby arithmetic is that?

He couldn't do it.

Farber might want to operate, Frances said. "It's the sort of thing you can't ignore."

Blackburn thought he should ask about the diagnosis, then a completely unrelated matter came to mind. He had to get out of town, and pretty quickly. He certainly couldn't linger. A house directly across the street from where he lived in Sheepshead Bay was being rehabilitated, turned from a residence into a dental clinic. He wanted to submit a bid on some of the inside work: rolling walls and trimming windows, nothing anymore elaborate than that, but if he were to do it he couldn't hang around Carlyle forever.

"Please," Frances said, "the whole hospital doesn't have to hear. Lower your voice."

Only when she said that did Blackburn realize he'd been shouting.

Taken back, embarrassed, he told Frances he was sorry.

As a young man Blackburn's hair had been a conventional shade of red. Now the hair was thinning and the color fading. The colorless hair on the back of his arms, when seen from a certain angle, was just the faintest orange.

"I think I'd like to take a shower, Marty."

He didn't want to make things difficult, but Blackburn immediately questioned the wisdom of that, saying it might be too much for her.

"I'm sure I'll feel better after a shower," she insisted. Her insistence struck him as especially odd considering her earlier behavior.

Then it became clear. He felt it in his bones. Frances had a deeper purpose: she was getting out of the way. Someone would be coming and he would be unable to avoid being alone in the room with whoever it was.

In fact that didn't quite turn out. Instead, when she was in the bathroom showering the phone began to ring.

He picked it up. "Hello."

"Can I speak to Mrs. Blackburn? This is Dr. Farber."

"Frances is in the shower now, Dr. Farber. This is her husband." He waited for a reaction; when there wasn't any he went on. "Frances told me about her problem."

"I see."

"And you're sure that's what she has?"

"Get a second opinion if that will make you feel better."

Blackburn ignored the tone.

"I noticed she has some trouble breathing."

"We're doing what we can."

"Look, let me ask you something. I don't know if you'll want to answer this, but I have to try. Knowing what you know, if you were Frances and you had what she had, what would you do?"

"I'd kill myself."

"Who am I talking to? Is this Kevin?"

"This is Dr. William Farber."

"You don't sound old enough to be a doctor."

"Mr. Blackburn, let me tell you something. On balance I don't get much satisfaction out of helping people. But this is what it's been given to me to do, so I do it. I can help heal people. We didn't want you coming to the hospital, you know."

"If you're telling me I'm no good for Frances—."

"There's a good deal of speculation that you're responsible for her condition."

"I'm not going to worry about that."

"Mr. Blackburn, Frances is my patient. You had something to do with this condition and I feel that gives me a certain latitude, or responsibility." He paused, then spoke with intensity. "You're going to listen to what I have to say."

Blackburn hung up.

It was time to go. However, Frances, wrapped in a white terry cloth robe, was just coming out of the bathroom.

"Did I hear the phone ring?"

"I hung up on your doctor."

"Marty." She looked directly at Blackburn. "Honestly, I don't understand you. Weren't you prepared for anything at all? You brought this on yourself by coming back here. What did you expect?"

"I'm sorry, Frances," he said as he moved toward the door.

The road was remarkably bumpy. Cunningham Avenue ran from the southern-most tip of the city of Carlyle clear to its northern outskirts, at which point it turned into U.S. 51. Walking on the shoulder of U.S. 51, Blackburn told himself, would increase anyone's sense of vulnerability, but because he invested his response with unusual significance, in one regard at least he was not just anyone: when semis powered past him he found the shudder that went through him reassuring. There, he said to himself, see, you don't want to die.

Then he heard water.

A drainage ditch running parallel to the highway appeared to be dry. Here, a mile or a mile and a half from the airport, he saw no other obvious place to look. This was very curious. He remembered when, with the exception of a few gas stations and a three-hole golf course, there had been nothing but farmland out here as far as the eye could see. Not so any more. Earlier he'd passed a stretch of automobile showrooms: Selby Motors, Gutowski Cadillac Buick, and the like; up ahead he saw a bowling alley; there were parking lots, and in the midst of all this development, fields that had once defined the landscape now seemed squeezed together, very nearly out of place.

That was a commonplace observation, of course, but at the same time he'd become aware of something else entirely. He wasn't making progress; he wasn't getting any closer to the goddamn airport. The idea of being stranded, though it made no sense whatsoever, was starting to get hold.

And still there was another thing. He had a sneaking suspicion he was holding something back. There was the disconcerting feeling that he'd just made an incredible mistake, yet the moment was somehow retrievable; whatever he'd done could be undone if only he could put his finger on it, and certainly when he got home the first thing he'd do would be settle his bill with the motel and there would be no trouble having them forward his overnight bag. It wasn't easy to acknowledge this but he had to, it was true: he'd been afraid it might be Kevin who'd confront him in the hospital room, afraid even though such fear had been utterly without foundation.

Maybe that was it. Maybe, like almost any rumor, this unfounded fear was having some residual effect.

Look, he told himself, keep walking and try your best to bear this in mind: anytime, absolutely anytime you go on a sentimental journey, which was what this trip had been, after all, you take a calculated risk.

He heard the water. There was nothing to be seen, however, except across the highway an abandoned Illinois Central railroad track. The airport was not that far away. Slowly he walked past a cluster of new houses set well back from the highway. Each house was, of all things, the color of nailpolish: ice blue, peach, like some of the stucco bungalows, he realized, near the West End Beach Club at the very tip of Sheepshead Bay. It would have made for conversation had Frances been here with him.

He focused on his future. There was movement, but goddamn it, there wasn't any progress. Unless he was badly mistaken that was a bridge up ahead. His future; he concentrated. No matter how he filled it in, no matter what particulars he filled it in with, he couldn't work it out satisfactorily. Perhaps because he didn't want to mislead himself. More likely he couldn't work his future out satisfactorily because a satisfactory future wouldn't meet his needs.

So odd, he thought, that he didn't remember passing over this bridge on the way into town.

Slippery when wet, the sign said. He started across. The bridge was swaying.

And he thought that he knew why.

Blackburn wasn't all that sure of this himself: Frances couldn't know it; the doctor had no way of knowing; but hadn't he returned to Carlyle and to Frances, hadn't he turned back to his past to verify the present, which was something that was certainly advisable to do from time to time, and of course now that he'd done it the goddamn bridge was swaying.

But he wasn't scared.

Experience, he believed, proved that events beyond anyone's control will occur: that was life. He did not believe in God; instead he believed in irony and look where that had gotten him. What he should have been doing all along was learning punctuation, then at least there might have been something for him to cling to as he struggled to maintain his balance on the bridge on U.S. 51.

Still, he wasn't scared.

The mid-November sky was low; metal expansion joints began to creak, and if, as he suspected, this was a dream, then it was a dream, he thought with a curious lack of emotion, from which there was no waking.

A Period of Grace

It all began with a call from my mother. A few hours earlier she'd taken my father to the hospital and now even as we spoke he was on his way to surgery.

Control yourself, I thought. Let her finish.

After not feeling quite right for a couple of days he'd been much worse this morning, so Dr. Silverman of the Belmont staff had her bring him right in.

I stared at the linoleum, took one step, another, a third, each step moving me away from the kitchen entrance where the wall phone was located until, with the coiled telephone wire suddenly taut, I could go no further, like an animal who's used up all the slack in his leash or chain.

When they got to the hospital his records were out, my mother said, and by the time she'd finished in Admissions he was being given a transfusion.

"A transfusion?"

"Dad's bleeding internally. They have to find out what's causing it."

This was like anything else, I told myself, just think clearly. My father had already had two heart attacks. "It sounds like this is some new kind of problem entirely. What do the doctors suspect?"

"According to Silverman they really aren't sure what the basic problem is. You know the way Dad can be. Once he heard that he became reluctant to let them operate, but they kept saying without operating he'd die in a couple of hours."

"My God."

"Can you imagine? Still Dad wouldn't budge. He had one answer for everything: I'm seventy-two years old. If you open me up I probably won't make it anyhow. Anyway, when Dr. Lansky, the surgeon, learned what was going on he said it could be a bleeding ulcer so okay Dad finally relented."

I had no brothers. I had no sisters and classes wouldn't start for two more weeks.

"Should I come in?" It was 1,000 miles from Level to Brooklyn.

After a brief discussion it was decided we'd speak again after the operation, then see where we stood.

I knew where I stood. This could complicate everything. I wasn't proud of myself for thinking that but in fact my opinion of myself had essentially formed; events sometimes confirmed and sometimes refuted but rarely altered that opinion, which was linked to the suspicion that aspects or sides of myself existed that I hadn't yet uncovered. It was a matter of feeling intensely unfulfilled at times; perhaps I was simply sensing unexplored potential or reacting to lost opportunities.

This was 1971 and I was thirty-one and whatever it was it certainly wasn't that I was down on myself because of the breakup with Carol. It wasn't *only* that anyway, although we'd lived together for six years.

Our breakup had been a long time coming and at Christmas when we really finally sat down to talk there had been very little left to talk about. The decision to part had been mutual.

Adjusting, though, had been difficult. Teaching helped; it got me out of myself, provided a respite. I even judged a story contest. Nevertheless, in the course of a lifetime there are times when one's thoughts turn to death in ways that they never before had, and that winter was my time. For the first time in my life I realized that, like museums and cultural events that you don't go to, it was a comfort simply knowing it was there and available just in case you ever wanted to take advantage of it.

Then spring arrived and by God I began bouncing back. The signs were unmistakable: everything from an inclination to again eat the right foods, like lentil soup and rice and beans—which meant a willingness to put myself out; I'd gone months without chopping an onion—to becoming less preoccupied with the particulars of the will I'd been thinking of having drawn up.

Then while gearing up for summer school, with a fall sabbatical in the offing, my mother called.

The flatness in her voice, which I heard immediately, told me the release I'd been hoping for would not be forthcoming. She fumbled around for a bit then said, "I don't know what to say, Alan. Dad came through the operation but after all this was major surgery." She hesitated. "They took out part of his stomach."

I waited for the follow-up: context, explanation, something. "And?"

"There was a tumor."

"I'll get a flight in first thing tomorrow."

"Alan, listen to me. Dad's in recovery and he's doing as well as can be expected. Right now all we can do is hope and pray. We both have to stay as calm as we possibly can. It's too soon for the doctors to know much."

Ultimately that was how we left it. I certainly didn't want it to appear as if I was going off half-cocked.

It was now late afternoon. I assumed thoughts of my father would crowd everything else out but instead a kind of mindless discord began to register. I began to pace. Space was limited since my apartment, which was in one of the older frame houses near campus, had only three rooms. I stopped at my desk, straightened some papers, then concentrated on the fading, water-stained living room wallpaper directly in front of me. It depicted a standard pastoral scene. There were trees on the bank of a winding stream in the foreground and off in the distance mountains and sky. There was a high ceiling, a wooden floor, leaded glass but finally it was the freestanding mirror off in the corner that held my attention: there I was, black kinky hair sticking out like stunted wings from either side of an otherwise balding head.

Goddamn it, I thought, why now? After a winter and spring of not writing I was finally writing again. Certainly nothing like that had ever happened to me before.

In many ways until the breakup with Carol my situation hadn't been too bad. Though I didn't have a name or career as a writer, at least I had credentials, a list of publications, and of the dozen stories I'd published, one, "The Object," had done reasonably well for itself, having been commented upon—"deftly crafted," "a cerebral narrative with a fine soul"—by the *Times* reviewer when it appeared, a year after its original publication in *Quarterly Review*, in an anthology of the preceding year's best stories. It had been reprinted twice more after that. And on the basis of achievement as modest as that I'd been accepted at Monadnock, an artists' colony, for a fall residency.

The fall seemed a long way off, however. I thought about going to Farrell's for a drink but finally that wasn't appealing. The impulse to call Carol was very strong. She, after all, knew the people involved. On the spur of the moment I dialed her number, then as her phone rang for the third time I hung up, thankful that she hadn't answered, and after that all I really wanted to do was go to sleep.

Early the following morning a call from my mother woke me.

"Alan, could you come in today? I have to make a decision and I need your advice."

"Sure."

"Dad's still bleeding. He's in intensive care."

"I'll be in as soon as I can, probably late this afternoon. Look," I said, "maybe we ought to hang up so I can get right to work on the ticket."

After I put the receiver back in the cradle a long breath, which I hadn't known I'd been holding in, escaped and it was recognizable, even to me, as a sigh. "Jesus," I said out loud, "Jesus Christ."

Then I called Ozark and arranged for a ticket on the 12:50 flight to LaGuardia. Prepare for the worst, I thought, though of course there was no longer any certainty that *the worst* meant death. Hadn't the worst now come to mean being mechanically maintained for a prolonged period in a comatose state? Suddenly I didn't want to stick with my own particular situation. I decided instead to explore the avenue of broader implications. Also it would be necessary to go to the bank. Had profit motive played a role in extending life, I wondered. From there it was only a stone's throw to *greed*, then I made the leap to Man's Nature, and on entering that thicket I found distraction almost possible.

At five to twelve a cab picked me up for the fifteen-minute ride to the airport. The noon sky was gray, that shade that appeared in sixteen- or nineteen-inch patches on the TV screen when the set was on but no picture was being transmitted. At the check-in counter they assured me that conditions for flying were excellent and shortly after that it was time to board.

My father had never seemed youthful to me. Single into his thirties, almost forty when I'd been born, he'd never seemed elderly either. Sick, yes, but never hobbled or feeble.

Which was surprising because as far back as I could remember his conversation had dwelled on the past, on living in Harlem, which had been Jewish back then, and safe, even classy; even Gyp the Blood, who'd always treat you to a danish and a cup of coffee, my father said, gave hardly any sign that in the end he'd fry at Sing Sing. Bang bang: World War I spent shooting pool in Hoboken. He served as a private at the procurement center in the Army Field Clerk's office and after discharge it was home to manage the one-clerk United Cigar Store on 123rd Street and 6th Avenue. Corned beef sandwiches cost a dime at that time; the *News* cost a penny and cigarettes were ten cents a pack. There was Roseland and vaudeville; the Palace headlined Eddie Cantor. Sophie Tucker, Al Jolson, Jackson, Clayton & Durante: any one of those acts could bring down the house and Smith & Dale: there's no one like them around anymore, he'd say. Chinese restaurants had bands in those days, and a dance floor. If you took a girl out the whole night would run you a dollar and a half, maybe a dollar seventy-five. That was the time to be alive in this country. He'd been saying that when I was twelve and thirteen, when he'd been in his early fifties, and he'd probably been saying it long before that.

My earliest recollection of him had to do with being on the receiving end of occasional stinging slaps, but aside from that the only physical contact between us that made an impression came after I was finished with the navy and college, even later, when I began returning to Brooklyn on a regular basis with this job at Level. By then he'd retired from his civil service job. Hello, I'd call, walking in, anyone home? Sitting in the living room, looking startled although I hadn't interrupted anything, he'd fumble a bit while lifting himself from his chair. I knew that he'd been waiting for me, and perhaps it was precisely that turn of events that startled him so.

In a ritual the formality of which never failed to please me we'd shake hands, but over time his hand had come to feel small in mine, which invariably took me back, as I was always taken by surprise by the authority exerted by my grip, which would lead to a moment of confusion and to safely skirt the rush of emotion that would come after that I'd turn away from him, toward the kitchen, toward my mother who'd be approaching, smiling, with her arms out.

Right now, I was thinking, this very minute, my father could be dead.

"Where to?"

"Belmont Hospital."

The cabdriver nodded, pulled the flag.

Belmont Hospital bordered Brownsville, which was less than a ten-minute drive from my parents' East Flatbush home. Whatever Brownsville had been sixty years ago when my mother had lived there as a child, now acting in accord with the laws of urban physics it was an inner-city slum, black, shattered, and ever-expanding.

What did one say about this one-time neighborhood hospital that some years back had affiliated with a university, that now enjoyed a reputation for experimental treatments and innovative devices: Don't go there at night, it's too dangerous. That's what my family had argued about with my mother the last time my father had been in the hospital, and the time before that too.

The Grand Central Parkway, which we'd take to the Interborough, curved easily, went past marinas and graded roadside areas.

"You stay on the Interborough to the last exit. That'll be Pennsylvania Avenue."

"Nine times out of ten you go to one of these out-of-the-way neighborhoods you're going to come back light," the cabdriver said.

I ignored that. I told him I'd just flown in from Level, Illinois, which wasn't too far from Chicago.

"Oh yeah? I went to corpsman school at Great Lakes. Man, I made out like a bandit in Chicago. Chicago was so full of hitters I couldn't believe it. In Brooklyn," he looked into the mirror to catch my eye, "what we call hitters, out of town you call them greaser chicks."

"I'm originally from Brooklyn."

"Yeah, well, if you've been away for a while you ain't going to recognize it. There's a war going on here," he said.

There was no need to ask between who.

"People are animals. People used to think Staten Island was the answer but I got a cousin who says it's the same out there."

Fifteen minutes later we pulled up in front of the hospital.

It is commonplace for people who never see flying saucers or throw the I-Ching to recall standing, in a sense, outside themselves, wholly detached, observing their own action and behavior. As the cab drove away something similar to that happened to me. I saw the boulevard as it would be had it been empty of all traffic, as a vast sweep of curving asphalt, and somehow the picture this made was not unfamiliar. Like so many dashes, white traffic lines ran parallel to narrow, curb-high pedestrian islands, which furthered the impression that the space had been carefully, intricately plotted—and the madness was, the boulevard was the product of a society without private autos, with only a dribble of traffic: police cars, limousines, the army.

I braced myself, walked past a young black man wearing a dashiki and sunglasses, then pushed through the revolving door.

In the lobby a uniformed security guard directed me to the third floor. A sign was posted: Intensive Care Unit. I followed the arrow to a corridor with a set of closed double doors that opened easily, and suddenly I was in a different country: silent, uncluttered and forbidding. There was a waiting room at the end of the corridor and there sitting off by herself with her hands in her lap and her head lowered was my mother. I entered quietly. "Mom."

"Alan," she said, looking up. "You're here already." She reached for my hand.

Fair skinned and small boned, my mother was almost fragile in appearance, but her fragility was deceptive. When it came to pushing heavy furniture around, to washing walls, she'd been strong, instructed by a powerful sense of things, of family no less than housework.

"Here, let me get a chair," I said, then I stepped away and pulled one over.

Ceil, an aunt, had left awhile back, knowing I was coming in. Even as she spoke my mother seemed distracted, twisted her fingers, looked down. I let her take her time, noticed that the crisscrossing lines in her face had deepened, had given her skin a kind of quilted texture. "When I got here this morning I found out Dad was still bleeding. They're talking about operating again."

"My God. Well, where does that leave things? We're obviously not back where we started."

"Of course not. First of all Dad's been operated on once already, plus now I'm the one who has to give permission and now we know that it's cancer."

"Cancer," I said. "I see."

She was nodding. "Lansky says he wants to wait for a report from the laboratory but Silverman came out with it right after the operation. There's a spot on the liver they couldn't touch plus they didn't get it all out of his stomach."

Silverman came out with it right after the operation. She'd known last night, I thought. Then I thought, This isn't the time to get angry about that.

"Is it, you know, curable?"

She shook her head. "No. If it was up to your father believe me he wouldn't let them touch him."

I asked in a quiet voice, "What will you do, will you sign?"

"What choice do I have? If the bleeding continues he'll bleed to death. Can I say no? Can I play God? I don't know what to do, Alan."

"When do they need a decision?"

"Silverman said by tomorrow morning. I'm just praying we'll get a break and the bleeding stops by itself."

"Yesterday, when they thought the bleeding had stopped, did anyone give you an idea how much time Dad has left?"

"The only one who wanted to talk about that was this one doctor—Davidson." She immediately made it clear she didn't care for him. "He has his own reasons for talking," she said. "He wants to give Dad treatments."

I heard her skepticism, which I shared. "Treatments? God, I don't even think Dad should be told what he has, but if he gets radiation or cobalt there's no way in the world we'll be able to keep it from him."

"That's what I said. Davidson answered he'll use a treatment with drugs and injections and pills. It's chemotherapy. He's a hematologist. I talked to him when, as you say, they still thought things had gone well. When I asked him, How much longer does my husband have, he told me his father-in-law had stomach cancer, like Dad the kind where they couldn't get it all out and he said that man lived two years after they found it." She hesitated. "If you could only trust them."

"Right. If."

"Alan, believe me, if your father could have two more years I'd be happy. I'd settle for a sick old man if that's all I can have."

"Of course that would be okay. Davidson said we could hope for that?"

"He said maybe." She blew her nose. "After all, he's not a young man and two years are two years."

I nodded then tried to be comforting, understanding full well I wasn't here to influence. As my mother said, as far as the decision went, What choice did we have? I was here because my presence was called for, which was gratifying.

Especially so because of the relationship my father and I had had. Prior to the 1960s it had been distinguished by coldness and squabbling. In 1971, though things had improved, my stance didn't sit well with him. Forces had been set in motion with which he was uncomfortable; everything seemed fluid; nothing was stable. Still, there had never been a real break between us; I'd always known he cared for me, and if at times I'd kept that understanding even from myself it was because it had served my purposes to do so, had, for instance, added some dimension to teenage life.

Now, because of the circumstance that had drawn my mother and me together, we fell silent. The wait became fatiguing. I went over to the bookcase that had been slapped against the wall and poked through the paperbacks on the top shelf; they were westerns and mysteries mostly, but then on the bottom shelf, which I kneeled to investigate, I saw some hardbound books, their cloth covers faded, the pages thick: a novel by Fannie Hurst, *Lummox*, then a primer: the kind of books that were occasionally given a second life in furniture stores where they did service on the tops of end tables and in credenzas.

"Mom, it's almost time."

Soon afterward a straggling, funereal procession of relatives and closest friends took shape in the corridor. At 5:35 a nurse came to the door of the ICU and let us in.

Insofar as one's sense of things had been shaped by space shots or perhaps science fiction, this rectangular room, this small ward with a single row of ten or a dozen beds watched over by a head nurse and her crew, was familiar, recognizable. It was gray and white and gleaming in here, postmodern, highly organized, monitors, dials and screens, an artificial environment, man made, windowless, the sort of secular enterprise a cardinal occasionally places his blessing on. But it as easily could have been a chamber half a mile underground, hollowed out of solid rock; that too would have a precise distribution of artificial light, that too would have been run with quiet pronounced efficiency.

As we walked toward the far end of the room I found myself withholding weight from my step. Like a child sucking the last drops of soda through a straw and only getting sound, so with her eyes closed an old woman in the bed I was passing breathed. From two beds beyond hers my father watched our approach with a sober lack of expression. Flat on his back, recognizable but not familiar, his eyes remained on my mother.

"Hi. See who's here?"

He started to nod.

"Sit down." My mother motioned me to a chair.

"Hello, Dad."

He raised his fingers a few inches. Still nodding he looked at my face, trying, I thought, to spot a reaction. By force of repetition the nodding, the greeting, took on additional meaning, became something of a statement, and I knew what he was saying. *That's right, I'm not in such hot shape, am I?*

A clear plastic urine bag hung at the side of his bed.

"Hello, Alan." It was a whisper.

When he opened his mouth individual strands of spit, like elastic, stretched from one lip to the other. His tongue was coated white, the lips cracked. Blood was going into one arm. Tubes inserted through his nose sucked fluid out of his stomach.

"How's the patient?" my mother asked. "Would you like a drink?"

A monitor sat on brackets high on the wall behind my father, who shook his head. Nevertheless my mother leaned over and put a straw into the glass of water on the table. By the time she picked the glass up his eyes had closed.

"We should get going," I said when I saw other people start to leave.

My mother stopped at the desk to ask about my father's condition. "Ware. The last bed."

"One second, Mrs. Ware," a nurse said. After checking a three-by-five card on the wheel file she walked to his bed, returned. "No, no change, I'm sorry."

Outside the hospital there was a hot dog vendor who apparently did no business. Elderly people in aluminum folding chairs and canvas beach chairs sat in front of the apartment house directly across the boulevard. As we came close they grew silent, followed us with their eyes. In their widowhood, in their decline, they were taking our measure. Not rudely, of course, not disrespectfully. After all, why shouldn't our passing still idle chatter? They know what it is, I thought, with their canes and pains and walkers and pacemakers they know about hospitals, they know about problems.

"Here," my mother said on the next block, handing me the car keys.

Telephone calls kept us occupied through much of the evening. In between we bathed and ate. I unpacked, got the bedding out of the hall closet and made up my bed. The evening ended with us sitting across from each other at the breakfast room table. "It's a good thing you can't look into the future," my mother said. She was in her housecoat drinking tea. "I can hardly believe this." She shook her head despairingly. "After what went on in his family—I can't begin to tell you how many times Dad said to me, I don't ever want to go through what Murray went through. Were you old enough to remember—?"

"Of course," I said, barely controlling the impulse to be short. "Mom, look, there's something we should talk about. It's really important for us to remember that Dad's very old-fashioned in certain ways." She looked as if she was going to say something but I went on. "Remember when I was in last time and I told Dad I need a hemorrhoid operation? I asked him if it had been painful when he had his and you know what he told me? Nah, it's not a painful operation. It's what's known as a dirty operation. That's it in a nutshell. When it comes to the body Dad has very old-fashioned attitudes, and cancer, my God, to him cancer's something that's almost unmentionable."

"I agree. You're right."

It was as if I'd wanted her to acknowledge some point of disagreement which, however, seemed not to exist, yet I felt it did.

"Look, I remember when he was in Belmont with the diverticulitis. He wouldn't even listen when those doctors told him that without a colostomy he wouldn't be able to go. It was like talking to a wall. They actually begged him."

"Well," I said, "pressure tactics don't work on Dad."

"I'll tell you something else. He's always had it in for doctors."

"Look, if we wanted to make a list of the people Dad's had it in for we could make some list. "How about middle-aged fat women in tight pants? Am I right? They'd lead the list in Dad's book."

"But isn't that ridiculous? A man as smart as your father"—she hesitated—"he's not educated but he's bright."

"I know that."

"But he never developed any sense of proportion. It's a pity on him that he never had a chance to go to school. When he was growing up the home atmosphere wasn't what it should have been. They didn't encourage him."

"That carried over too, didn't it? Remember how Dad used to tell me school's a lot of malarkey? Remember when he used to tell me that?"

"It pleased him when you finally went to college."

"How about when I went into the navy?"

"That was strictly your decision. We saw you meant it so we respected it." She looked away. "Your father's always been concerned about two things—his appearance and having a roll of bills in his pocket."

"In other words, under that veneer maybe there's a little inferiority complex."

There was a long silence, then, shaking her head as if remembering, she said, "Could that man dance. All you had to do was give him the chance. I'll say this, he's the one who deserves the credit for keeping me youthful. If it wasn't for his encouragement believe me I'd never buy the clothes I buy. He liked my figure. Thank God for small favors.

"Alan, I don't say those proctologists weren't sincere, but they like to lay it on a little bit. Patients have to think for themselves. We can't just accept what they tell us. That's why I can't help thinking, Dad fooled them before, maybe he'll fool them again. Dr. Harris—you remember her I'm sure"—I nodded—"she works on an Indian reservation now. You knew that, didn't you? Anyway, she gave us a diet and after all it's six years later and he's still here even though those doctors swore that couldn't happen."

There was the beginning of a smile, but it faded. And after a pause she said, "At least we have until tomorrow."

"What time should we be there?"

"First thing. The office opens at eight."

There was no temptation to close the bedroom curtains, not tonight. I lay under a single loose sheet discovering with gratitude that I was exhausted. Under the weight of this exhaustion I began to feel myself sinking, nearing sleep. Then, imperceptibly, it leveled off; a slight resistance, which I could ignore for only so long, set in, increased to restlessness. Movement became necessary. I began to raise my knees and in the midst of doing that, acting rashly, out of a sense of frustration and perversity, to have it over with, I sank the heels of both feet into the mattress, then ran them back and forth until my skin actually burned and my breath came in spurts.

This left me close to trembling. There. Good. Fuck it. That settled that. I reached for the radio, turned it on, then shut it right off. Unable to stand a thing on my skin I kicked the sheet away, turned to the other side of the bed, curled up and stared out into the living room. Then it hit me: the bleeding was going to stop. Of course I wanted it to, but what if it did? I was looking ahead.

As if badly sunburned I felt hot and chilled at the same time. Who would tell my father what he had, I wondered, then my mind raced on and it wasn't until I found myself half-raised in bed, eyes open and straining but without direction or intent, that I realized I'd fallen asleep. I let myself drop back to the pillow and so the night passed for me, fitfully, in starts and jerks.

My mother and I entered Silverman's basement office at exactly 8:15 the following morning. We approached his secretary with something like religious solemnity.

"Would you tell Dr. Silverman we're here. I'm Mrs. Ware. I'm supposed to speak to him about my husband."

"Mrs. Ware, I'm awfully sorry," this secretary with frosted hair said, "but Dr. Silverman's not in right now." Smiling, she held her face at an upward tilt. "Could I help you?"

It took my mother a moment to respond. "No," she said, "I'm supposed to talk to *him*."

The secretary maintained her smile, nor was there any change in the upward tilt of her face. A half-filled styrofoam coffee cup, the brim of which was smudged with lipstick, stood next to a typewriter. Otherwise the desk was clear.

The phone rang.

After answering it the secretary turned back to us and when she spoke there was warmth in her voice. "That was Dr. Silverman, Mrs. Ware. Your husband stopped bleeding early this morning. He'll be down here in fifteen or twenty minutes. Why don't you have a seat."

"Thank God," my mother said as we moved away, "thank God." We sat down. "Alan, I'm so relieved I just can't tell you."

"Same here," I said, but in fact, as I thought of what lay in store for my father, I had to back off.

"Look, it's almost visiting time. Go upstairs and see Dad. I'll wait here."

"Okay." I could see where Silverman might say, Dave, I'm sorry to tell you this but I have some bad news for you. And I could imagine him saying, You have cancer. But that was it. I simply could not go on from there. None of the predictable or stock responses, or variations on those responses, fit, and I wouldn't indulge my apprehension by conjuring up mad or fearsome things.

Positive it would soon be upon us, that scene and then his life as it would be lived under the influence of that knowledge loomed as a formless, frightening blank.

His eyes were open.

"How you doing, Dad?"

The gleaming silver sidebars were raised on either side of the bed, enclosing him. He looked as he had the night before, but there was a lack of curiosity there which I was afraid would not extend as far as it might, to the point of placing him beyond surprise.

"I had a close call."

"Mom told me. She's downstairs waiting for Silverman."

"Did mother tell you"—he took a breath—"I was bleeding internally?"

"A bleeding ulcer's not the kind of thing you want to fool around with." He didn't have any response. "I guess they treat you pretty well up here."

"They don't know if you're dead or alive."

"Oh yeah?" I laughed as if his intention had been to amuse me but his tone had been flat, without inflection. And soon after that I said, "Well, I better be going. You want me to get anything for you?"

He shook his head.

It was easy to imagine how Silverman would see me—with contempt: bearded, in Levis and sandals, a marginal type he wouldn't have to take into account, so how could I think he'd accede to our wishes, reverse himself, give us what we wanted. I punched Basement, got off the elevator, then as if long familiarity with this basement made arrival at Silverman's office inevitable, I proceeded without regard to the forks or cutoffs that appeared in my path; I simply went where my feet took me, excoriating him. Until something began to impinge. People were standing in the corridor in small noisy groups, smoking, drinking coffee, listening to radios, laughing. Janitors, maintenance workers, kitchen help, the people who did the shitwork here. There were no medical people here, no visitors cutting through this corridor lighted as poorly as a tunnel with its cinderblock walls, uncovered airducts, and low-hanging pipes that made a hazard of the ceiling. I was aware of the studied indifference, if not the hostility, of the people I was passing. Where had I wandered? It was like enemy territory. I passed an open freight elevator filled with barrels of trash. Unattended canvas carts loaded with laundry lined a stretch of corridor and finally seeing no way out I approached a woman from the kitchen staff and asked for directions, which she gave in a West Indian accent that was so heavy I couldn't understand her.

"Where have you been?"

"I got lost. The damn place is huge."

Before any kind of conversation started the secretary called us, ushered us into Silverman's office, which was surprisingly dumpy. He was on the phone. We sat in chairs on either side of his desk, free for the moment to look at the diplomas and photographs all over the walls. One of the photos was of a barefoot man in a striped polo shirt and rolled-up dungarees. The slight middle-aged man who was winding up this phone conversation bore little resemblance to that beachcomber; neither did he bear much resemblance to the person pictured on the deck of the cabin cruiser wearing a yachting cap. In fact, he was convincing only as the unpictured father of the adolescent girl in full riding habit standing beside a huge brown horse.

"Just one more second," Silverman said, hanging up, making a note on his desk calendar.

"Dr. Silverman," my mother finally said, "I don't know if you've ever met my son, Alan."

We shook hands. Then she asked if he knew how long my father would be staying in Intensive Care.

"I'd like to keep him there about a week. We think the bleeding stopped—."

"You think?"

"It slowed down, we know that, but we can't give 100 percent assurances. There was some blood in his stool earlier in the morning. That's not unusual, believe me. Maybe it was old stool, or maybe there's some seepage, but even if there is that's the sort of thing that can be controlled."

"Okay."

"I want to assure the both of you that Dave's not in much discomfort right now."

"Dr. Silverman," I said, "I wonder if you could tell me just exactly what the situation is."

"Your father has cancer. Unfortunately it can't be treated surgically.

I guess your mother told you Dr. Davidson would like to start him on chemotherapy."

"Can that cure him?"

He shook his head. "It might shrink the tumor for a while or retard its growth. . . ."

"That's what I thought. How much time would you say my father has left?"

"I can't tell you that."

"What bothers us is the idea of having my father go through more than is absolutely necessary. In other words, our goal is to see him stay as comfortable as possible for as long as possible." Silverman's face didn't reveal anything. "What about side effects?"

"Generally there's nausea, weakness, nothing terrible, but I wouldn't say it's pleasant. Some patients lose their hair. There could be a strong reaction but as I say, reactions can be controlled."

"Dr. Silverman, I don't think this would be a good thing for my father. You know, if it was up to us he wouldn't even be told what he has."

He seemed surprised. "Why do you say that?"

My mother spoke up. "You saw the way Dave was when he came in. He's not anxious to become involved with a lost cause."

A small bulb attached to the base of his desk phone started to blink. He picked up the receiver. "Yes." And then: "Let me get back to you in a few minutes." He turned to us again. "I'm sorry. Go ahead."

At this point I began to have hope. We repeated ourselves, said that given my father's attitude the damage that would be done by following the course he was suggesting was greater than any good that might come from it.

How to explain Silverman's shift? It was my guess that he was predisposed in certain directions: that he had a standard response to the kind of condition my father had: we'll doctor it as best we can. Of course, he knew there existed a wide range of response to news of terminal illness, and since our response fell within that range he wasn't entirely put off. He could adjust to it.

"Mrs. Ware, there's going to be a meeting of the cancer board in a couple of days. That's a group of staff doctors who go over every one of our cancer cases and make certain determinations. You're sure you feel the way you do?" He looked from my mother to me.

We nodded.

"Then taking into account what I know of the patient, I'm going to recommend against treatment until such time as the cancer starts causing discomfort." Neither one of us said a word. "After hearing what the two of you said, I'm not really convinced that treatment at this time would be in Dave's best interest."

"Are you saying that for a while Dad's not going to have any discomfort?"

There was something grudging or reluctant about the way in which he said, "That's right, for a while."

As far as I was concerned, now it was simply a matter of getting out of the office before he took it all back. He and my mother were talking, then they were standing, she was saying: "And as far as time goes you don't want to make a guess, is that it?"

"If you want to put it that way."

"Dr. Silverman, thanks," I said, and again we shook hands.

Outside the office my mother and I looked at each other: a reprieve: no treatment. Already I could feel the breathing room this gave me. There would be a pain-free period, a period of grace.

When we went back to my father a few hours later his color had improved. He seemed to gain ground all through the day. Late in the afternoon he asked that the next time we come we bring him his radio, his glasses, and a package of hard candies.

On the way home my mother said, "He can snap back. We know that about him."

She used the very same words when talking to relatives on the phone that night. Then we ourselves talked about it some more.

"Dad's plucky," I said. "In his own way he's a fighter."

"In his own way is right. When he wants to fight, then he's a fighter."

When we arrived the following morning our spirits were incalculably higher than they'd been twenty-four hours earlier. My father was sitting at the edge of his bed swinging his legs; the tubes were out; his teeth were in. I somehow felt he was putting on a show. The gristled fold of flesh hanging from his chin to his neck, though slack, had a certain sharpness to it, a quivering edge. Even that signified something positive to me. And then after he lay back down his questions to us were about getting out of intensive care and when he'd come home.

His progress continued. We alerted the family to the fact that we didn't want him to learn he had cancer. There was a second conversation with Silverman, this one in front of a supply closet in the corridor outside of intensive care. My father was going to be moved to a semi-private room that afternoon, Silverman said. We were delighted. We told Silverman how pleased we were with the progress my father was making and with the care he was receiving. Then he said that actually his purpose in talking to us was so that we could look ahead a little.

"When Dave gets home—."

"Which should be when?" my mother asked.

"I'm only guessing but I'll say in about ten days. Let him do whatever he feels up to doing. Try to go back to your normal routine."

"Wonderful," my mother said. "And as far as diet, is there anything in particular that he shouldn't have?"

"I'd follow the same rule. Let Dave more or less lead the way."

"Dr. Silverman, what about time?"

"No one can say precisely. It could be anything from a few months to a year or more."

I saw my mother struggling to maintain her composure. We hadn't been prepared for that. The rest of the conversation we simply rode out, nodding automatically, agreeing when he said, "Somehow or other you all have to return to your normal routine."

We were left very much subdued by the possibility that my father only had a few months left. Nevertheless, that night my mother and I had a discussion which Silverman's discussion with us made legitimate or permissible. Evidently we were not going to be faced with a critical period immediately. One stage had been completed and there was no point in our going on as if I could stay here indefinitely. The next morning we spoke to my father, he agreed, and suddenly I was making plans to leave.

Only six blocks from my campus office, my apartment in Level was in a residential neighborhood whose character had changed considerably in the last several years. From early in the century up to World War II and even beyond, a smattering of the town's substantial citizens, lawyers, and businessmen and the like, had lived here comfortably, unpretentiously, in the particular style of the time and place, and since the neighborhood houses varied in size, as did the plots of land on which they stood, it was apparent that people of modest means had lived here too: the GP setting up his first practice, for instance, someone connected with the railroad, perhaps the bank cashier.

It wasn't hard imagining it as it had been. The ample, unadorned front porches, most the kind that wrapped around a side of the house assuring a breeze on all but the stillest of summer nights, spoke of hominess: of people who raised families and knew their neighbors, people who, though wary of frills, maintained whatever was theirs and assumed others would do the same, who expected to die if not in the house then at least in the town in which they'd long lived. That, I thought, was how it had been.

Now it was different. Now, as registration for summer session began, hedges that had once been a border for front yards edged well over the narrow sidewalk, forcing couples and groups of three into single file as they walked by. On many of these two- and three-story frame houses a clanking patchwork of mailboxes covered an area of wall next to the front door; that and the chained bicycles on the porch told the story: of homeowners who sold to realtors who cut the houses up into rooms and apartments then rented them out to students, dropouts, and younger faculty. The results were predictable. Paint was flaking off the exterior of house after house after house. Instead of standing straight up and down, the white columns holding up a porch roof often leaned or slanted, sometimes in opposite directions, so that even if weeds hadn't been coming up through cracks in the cement, even if curbstones that needed replacing had been replaced, it still would have been obvious that the area was running down. In a rundown, overgrown way it had taken on a seedy appearance. I was comfortable here, and confident I'd pick up right where I left off. I'd teach; I'd write; I wouldn't look for a relationship, though, just a little action, that would be plenty.

I began by starting to move, inch by hostile inch, through the story I'd been on. And I stayed in close touch with Brooklyn. Then, on the night of the first day of summer school, after sitting out on the porch drinking gin and tonics and catching what breeze there was, I started feeling antsy, went for a walk, ended up in Carlson's ordering pizza and a draft. The enrollment in my summer class was small. At least keeping my father from knowing he had cancer was causing no moral dilemma: I didn't see it as a matter of right and wrong. There was only one concern: could we keep it from him. There was a related concern too: that I proceed cautiously, though I wondered if *proceeding cautiously* wasn't just a less obvious kind of overreaction. Stop that, I thought, please adjust, just adjust: as if there were a set of dials on me that I ought to be able to turn until got I myself exactly right, but that wouldn't happen and I knew why: because crazy as it was, deep down I was actually blaming myself for this having happened. Whoa, I thought, that really is insane. You don't run the world.

Then the waitress brought the pizza. When I said thanks she smiled at the tabletop, which I couldn't understand. Hadn't she met my eye when I'd first come in and ordered? I knew good and well that she had. Then it dawned on me that ever since then I'd been staring at her in a mindless, dogged way, shifting about in my booth, in fact, so that I could follow her with my eyes when she made trips to the kitchen and back.

Embarrassed, humiliated, I wanted to get out of there. I knew what was going on. This was the kind of unsatisfactory, remorseless half drunk I seemed to have a goddamn patent on, the kind that would turn on me before I was even through with it. No wonder I had to hold myself in check. No damn wonder.

On the way home my mood changed and I stopped at Farrell's.

Perhaps it was inevitable that I gravitated toward the kind of summer party you might stop at because someone at a bar had mentioned it was being given, where as soon as you turned the corner you knew which house to go to, the kind which if you were a neighbor you'd want to call the police on.

I was in the kitchen of the house at 608 East Vine; earlier in the evening a bartender at Farrell's had mentioned a party was going on here and it was open.

As sometimes happens in the Midwest when the peas are being passed one way and the butter the other, joints were going around in a clockwise and counter-clockwise direction simultaneously.

"Good shit," someone said. I took a hit.

But I didn't feel comfortable. The times were such that certain younger individuals were allowed to see themselves as an entirely new quantity and among them were some who were engaged by only the most remote of ideologies and faiths. From that bedrock position, in one form or another, as social allies or political affiliates, co-opted or unredeemed, it was all counter-culture here.

"Look who's here."

I turned, and there among the granny glasses, headbands, and bandannas, uncharacteristically sauced and wonderfully military in a much too large navy blue band jacket with a double row of brass buttons that some member of the university's marching band had once worn, was Carol.

"How you doing?" I asked.

She raised an open hand and placed it lightly on my chest. Had this been a movie I would have fallen backward, a corpse. Instead Carol moved, slipped her other hand behind me, in effect wrapping her arms around me.

"Alan," she said, "I'm so stoned I can't believe it." Then she bounced away. "Let's dance."

We made our way to a dark and crowded room that was empty of furniture. Afterward, sitting together on the porch steps in back, I said, "So you're doing okay?"

"I have my ups and downs. I guess I've been down for a while."

"If I'd known that," I said, "I would have given you a call. You should have called me, Carol."

"How's your father?"

"You heard about him?"

"I ran into Bill Mattingly. He told me."

She knew the whole story. "The only thing I can think to do," I said, "is go about business as normally as possible. How about you? How's your job?"

"Are you kidding?" We both laughed. She worked in the university's information office writing news releases, doing publicity. They were shorthanded and overworked, the usual problems.

Then silence followed and a certain amount of tension built up. She finally broke it.

"How are your hemorrhoids?"

"God, come on, Carol."

"Okay, well, let's see. I met Denise's shrink at her Fourth of July party and guess what, I got shrunk."

"That must have been a thrill."

"Don't be so uptight. It was really interesting."

"What did he find out?"

"Nothing that I didn't know, that I don't have a strong self-image, that I let people take advantage of me, the same old stuff."

I rubbed my forehead with two fingers as if I had a headache. Later in the evening we returned to my apartment. Then, first thing in the morning, pale and severe, Carol told me that I'd caught her at a low point, this changed nothing, sometimes she was depressed, period.

"Don't you even want to stay for breakfast?"

"I just want to go home. Please, Alan, don't try to make anything out of this."

"Why would I?" I said. "I'm not a glutton for punishment. We're not viable, I know that," but her instincts had been right and the temptation had been there.

According to my mother, my father had been having his ups and downs. I wanted to go back to Brooklyn and see for myself just how he was doing. It was a matter of peace of mind.

At the time it seemed I'd be able to get away for a long weekend the third week of July, so I made a round-trip reservation, then I began to wonder what exactly was working on me. Love, and guilt, I insisted on that, and in addition to that I was moved by his vulnerability.

At least I was satisfied with the hours I was spending writing. In a perverse moment I toyed with the idea of doing a *father dying* story but common sense dictated that before an experience be turned to fiction it be allowed to fully unfold. I even had a title: *Life Without Father*.

I couldn't shake the idea. I would realize, at odd moments, when I thought I was thinking about something else, that I was actually trying material out on myself. But I was nothing if not analytical and it was abundantly clear that I couldn't write my father's story with any kind of authority, not now. It was abundantly clear I didn't even know what his story was. It was equally clear that something had to be done. I decided to come at the thing indirectly, by committing to paper some thoughts that might have a bearing. I'd do it with the idea of ending up with one of those curious odds and ends whose proper place is in a writer's notebook.

The inescapable, irrefutable truth was that my ambition as a writer extended even to that. In the proper frame of mind I could imagine myself translated, interviewed, thought of as an influence. In that frame of mind I could imagine that someday notebooks, scraps, my very thoughts might be found to be of interest.

First I came up with a title:

Thoughts Regarding Common Sense
as Common Sense Pertains to Fiction

After struggling I started it out in just the right academic tone:

> Fiction isn't charged with recreating, merely with embodying reality. In addition to telling a story and revealing character, fiction that somehow makes accessible some aspect or facet of reality that reality, because of its particular configuration, keeps inaccessible, outdoes itself, transcends itself.
>
> For instance, imagine real life. Imagine (in real life) approaching a long-term convict or a misshapen cripple. Just imagine telling either one that he's Symbolic, a Metaphor for Modern Man. Assume that while telling him this you're well fed, well paid, free as a bird, yet you tell him that he Represents you. You tell him he's Everyman. He is everyone currently living beyond hospital walls.
>
> Though that will outrage common sense, what you're saying will have some merit. Most likely, though, it will not be in real life but in finely

focused fiction, in fiction that sees through the apparent, that harsh realities like that will be most convincingly revealed.

It occurred to me, after reading that, that I was out to enlarge upon my father in the story I might someday write. I'd extend him, inflate him, heighten him. That was perfectly clear. But what was it that he might become the embodiment of? Schoolwork kept me from getting to that. It kept me from making the trip back to Brooklyn, too, which, luckily, I hadn't mentioned to my parents because I'd known all along there was a chance I might have to postpone it. It was fitting, I thought, that in fiction I seemed to want to blow my father up while in life I saw him as reduced.

Ironically, on the Monday of the third week in July—the week I'd originally intended to go to Brooklyn—my officemate, Bill Mattingly, called, "Alan, for you."

He held out the phone. It was my mother. The news was grim, incomplete.

After a couple of days of severe pain my father had again entered the hospital. They'd drawn fluid from his lungs, she said, and taken a sliver of bone out of his back. It was too soon to come to any conclusions.

But when I spoke to Bill he agreed:

"This is the start of it," I said. "I'll bet anything." The next day confirmation came: the cancer was spreading.

Silverman told my mother we were now at the stage where chemotherapy was in order, but it couldn't start for a while, not until a series of tests had been completed.

Both my mother and I realized that if my father didn't know what the tests were for he'd resist them.

Starting the second night my father and I spoke regularly. I listened to his complaints. He agreed that getting the fluid off his lungs had given him some relief but otherwise it was all a bunch of hooey. They were x-raying him from top to bottom for what: It knocked him out and ran up a bigger and bigger bill. On the other hand Silverman was arguing with my mother that my father should be told what he had, maybe then he'd stop fighting him every step of the way. On the fourth day of my father's hospitalization Silverman gave my mother an ultimatum: You tell him or I will, the result of which was, Silverman was going to speak to my father the following morning. I told my mother that before Silverman told Dad he had cancer I wanted to speak to Silverman.

I reached him at his office at 8 A.M. I asked if he couldn't say the chemotherapy was necessary for a stomach problem. That way my father would see a reason for the tests and he'd probably cooperate.

"Mr. Ware, I think that up to this point I've met you and your mother more than halfway." I didn't answer. "Did you ever stop to think that maybe your father wants to know what he has?"

"I think I know my father."

"Alan, I'm asking you to trust my judgment."

There was no way I could answer that. The rest of the morning passed, the afternoon passed. That night, filled with apprehension, I called my mother.

"Alan," she said, "it was the most amazing thing." And for a moment I thought, My God, he handled it.

As it turned out it wasn't quite that way. During her afternoon visit my father behaved as if nothing was different, so she'd assumed Silverman had postponed the talk; but when she checked at his office she found that no, he had indeed spoken to my father.

"So you're saying Dad knows he has cancer?"

"If he knows I couldn't tell it," my mother said, "and that's not like Dad."

"Well, did he or didn't he agree to the chemotherapy?"

"There's still some testing left to do so Silverman didn't ask for a yes or no."

I wanted to call my father immediately; maybe then I'd be able to make sense of this but my mother prevailed: he might need time to himself, she said, wait until tomorrow.

The next night as soon as my father answered the phone I could tell he had something to say.

"How did things go today?"

"Typical," he said, "typical." They hadn't brought him his breakfast. That was the one meal of the day he could stomach, so he called the nurse who told him he was scheduled for a barium enema in half an hour. He wanted to know why he hadn't been told about that in advance, and missing breakfast was going to make him weaker, not stronger: that's what he told her. The upshot of the whole thing was the nurse walked out, then Silverman called and said this would be the last test, then they could start chemotherapy.

"I told him I wasn't going to take it. The first time I ever heard the word chemotherapy was yesterday."

"What did he say?"

"According to Silverman that's the only thing they can do for me so I said if that's the case I might as well go home so that's how it stands. Mother's coming to get me tomorrow morning."

"Dad, do you feel this is the right thing to do?"

"Sure."

"Let me ask you something. Did Silverman say *why* you need this treatment?"

"He says I have a tumor, and as far as treatment this is what they recommend. It's some kind of intravenous deal with injections right into the blood. It's hard to understand. Don't worry about it."

His tone betrayed no anxiety. I didn't feel he was putting me off, but the response itself was off, too casual. I didn't buy it. On the other hand I didn't feel I could bore in, corner him, and perhaps shatter some fragile construction of his own making.

When I called my mother she asked if I was certain he'd used the word *tumor*. Yes, I said, he had. I asked if he was in shape to come home.

"I don't know," she said.

"What about medicine, and there's something else, is he going to be able to get back into Belmont? I mean sooner or later he'll have to, won't he?" She didn't answer. "This is scary. Is he even under a doctor's care anymore?"

"Alan, I just don't know."

The next night when I called home I heard that my father was up and around. It sounded as if it was manageable.

A few days later I called when my father was napping. My mother told me a neighbor from across the street, Anna Marino, had dropped by the second or third day Dad was home. "You know Dad. He began complaining about the runaround the hospital gave him, and the bills—which really are impossible. So Anna asked him, With all the testing they did, did they ever find out what's wrong with you? His answer was, They think it's some kind of blood disorder. When I heard that I'm telling you, Alan, I almost dropped."

"A blood disorder. Jesus Christ. That's incredible. My God, Mom, does he know or doesn't he?"

"How can he not know?"

"You know something"—this came out before I knew what I was saying—"he knows and he doesn't know. Maybe this is what Dad has to do to face it."

From the way my mother went on I could tell she wasn't impressed. It was almost as if in the face of this overwhelming reality explanations were superfluous, irrelevant. But it made good sense to me.

"Anyway, I'm definitely coming in next weekend."

The five-and-a-half-room semi-detached brick house in which my parents had lived for most of their marriage, in which I'd grown up, had been built in the 1920s at a time when East Flatbush was barely developed, when the nearest subway station was on Eastern Parkway and Utica Avenue and it took a twenty-five-minute trolley ride to get there, when corner lots on residential side streets were going begging. It had been built at about the time the first stand of businesses had been established on Avenue D: a grocery, of course, and a couple of taverns and a tailorshop with a tailor who lived behind it; there was a dry goods store, a bakery, then hardware and candy stores. Yet even later, much later, after the lumberyard had burned down, when the movie house opened, still many of the side streets remained unpaved, which curiously enough was what was in the back of my mind as I shook hands with my father and kissed my mother and then carried my luggage into the bedroom. I could remember when certain side streets in this neighborhood had been unpaved: that seemed as improbable to me as the fact that my mother could remember when there had been farms in Brownsville.

It was chilly out, windy, as if a storm was coming up, but the house was warm. Still my father was bundled in sweaters, his belt pulled to the last notch, his pants bunched at the waist. Judging by outward appearances, though, he was still in fairly reasonable shape.

"School's over now?" my father asked.

"Right." We spoke about what I might expect at Monadnock. I saw that he didn't eat much of supper but he did eat some of everything. I asked him, "How's the neighborhood holding up?"

"Don't get him started," my mother said.

"The politicians wrote Brooklyn off a long time ago. As soon as they do that it's all over."

He went on and I didn't argue.

Later, after my father had gone to bed, when my mother and I were alone, I asked her how she was holding up under the strain. During the next few days I came to understand something about living at the brink, at the precipice. You find, she told me, you don't live for each day. You can't. Even though the question *When will it happen?* was always uppermost, you begin, after living with uncertainty for a time, to adjust to it. Each day became like the day before.

"And you think," I asked my mother my first night home, "Dad's not losing ground?"

"Look, healthy he's not but so far so good."

I returned to Level knowing it couldn't last much longer.

Officially my sabbatical would begin when the fall semester began; unofficially it was already underway, but I couldn't get down to the serious business of writing. This was an in-between period; I'd leave for Monadnock in two weeks.

As I made the arrangements a kind of destructive mood descended. He would die.

He would die. That was the Ultimate Revision. What else could be said in behalf of death. At least it wasn't just another phase we passed through. What would I do if, like something with a continuous surface that folds back on itself, the meaning of his dying was self-contained, enclosed, simply wrapped up in itself? Lower my sights, perhaps, and settle for the drama.

Then five days before I was scheduled to leave the call that had to come came from my mother. My father had been readmitted to Belmont early that day.

"Who made the arrangements?"

"Dad. He did everything. He made the call, he did the talking. I stayed out of it completely."

Even as we talked I began looking ahead, as if rehearsing what was to come so I'd handle it smoothly.

Actually this created only a minimal amount of inconvenience. I canceled one flight, booked another. Good-byes had to be said in any event. I notified Monadnock, gave them my Brooklyn telephone number and address.

I scanned the hospital lobby but my writer's eye failed me. All I saw were the things anyone would see: the bank of public telephones in the alcove, the giftshop, the empty holster the security guard wore as part of the uniform. Well, I thought, what could you expect. This was one of the hottest, muggiest days of the year.

"Six, please." Nothing could be done for my father; that was a cold hard fact. I wondered what the chances were of having him transferred from the semi-private room my mother said he'd been assigned to, to intensive care where, if nothing else, I felt they always went all out.

But that was ridiculous. A life wasn't at stake, a life was ending. In that situation all *going all out* could mean was providing my father with the attention necessary to assure what little ease might be possible.

On the sixth floor patients in bathrobes and slippers were strolling to and from the lounge. Television sets seemed to be playing in half of the eighteen or twenty rooms that lined this corridor. I resented this normal activity. Somehow it seemed inappropriate to the gravity of my father's condition.

"Look who's here," my aunt said the moment I stuck my head in the doorway.

My smile traveled, took in my parents as well as Ceil, this sweetest of aunts who was seated in a chair at the foot of the bed holding her round, pretty face up to be kissed, her fingers, swollen with rings, light on my wrist as I bent over and brushed her cheek.

Short and plump with bracelets and a necklace and tiger orange hair, there was now a series of hairline cracks, like the markings on a ruler, on the skin of Ceil's upper lip.

My father said hello then asked the standard first question. "How was your trip in?" His voice sounded unusually thick.

"Easy, no trouble at all."

My mother pointed, directed my attention to an elderly woman sitting at the side of the third bed in this three-bed room. The elderly woman was pointing to an empty chair beside her, indicating to me that I should take it so that I too might sit.

I waved away the offer. Because of the room's heat the covers only came to my father's knees then doubled back. Conceivably I'd overreacted; perhaps he wasn't on the verge of dying. His temples were hollowing though and his cheekbones, which had never before been prominent, now stuck out.

"What's all that?" I pointed at a device my father had on that looked much like a swimmer's noseclip.

"Oxygen. When the doctor was in he showed Dad how to use it."

"Silverman was in?" I immediately regretted saying that because it could be misinterpreted. It wasn't a reference to hard feelings that might exist on Silverman's part toward a patient who'd essentially walked out on him. I assumed that had been resolved.

"No, some kid," my father said.

"You'll meet him," my mother said. "He's nice, isn't he Ceil, Dr. Bloom?"

For some reason my father's face wasn't a shock. I wasn't measuring him against the way he'd been but against an image, which so far eluded me, of the way I feared he yet would be.

The gaunt, gray-haired man who until now had been lying quietly in the middle bed suddenly began talking; stiff backed, gesturing, he sat straight up and threw his covers off. Then the words abruptly stopped and he fell back like dead weight. Without covers, with the white hospital gown bunched at his waist, I could see that his right leg ended in a stump above the knee and he wore diapers.

In the absolute silence that followed I hesitated, reluctant to look at my father, fearful of his reaction. In fact there was a bland expression on his face as he turned the dial on his transistor radio as if what went on in the next bed was no concern of his and it wasn't until Ceil started speaking—I had no idea what she was saying—that he put the radio aside. Five minutes later she said it was time she got going.

"So," Ceil asked with unavoidable solemnity as I walked her to the elevator, "how does Dad look to you?"

I was surprised to find I couldn't answer her; his appearance hadn't shocked me yet I couldn't get the words out. All I could manage was a shrug.

"Where are you going?" my mother asked.

My father was struggling to sit up, shifting weight from one elbow to the other, in that way raising his body little by little.

"Do you want to go to the toilet?"

"Yeah."

After managing to raise himself he got his legs over the side. Next he inched his body to the edge of the bed, pressed his palms into the mattress, tried to stand. His knees buckled. In the instant that it took me to reach out and grab him he steadied himself and I realized I had no choice: I had to take my hand away.

Standing on his own, breathing hard, he said, "Goddamn it, it catches me right here." He pointed to his chest.

My mother and I, spectators, stared as he started toward the bathroom, shuffling, his feet barely leaving the ground, his shoulders so round his pajama top rode up his back the way a sweatshirt does after it shrinks.

"My God, Mom," I whispered after the door closed, when we could hear him urinating, "how much does Dad weigh?"

She put her finger to her lips silencing me.

"We should be going soon."

"Alan, are you coming back tonight?" my father asked.

"Of course."

The squat, sturdy woman who'd earlier offered me a chair had posted herself in the corridor. She was watching hall traffic, keeping tight hold of her knitting bag, ignoring the cry of "Shirley, Shirley" coming from the patient in the third bed, although earlier, at his bedside, she'd talked, pleaded, cajoled: Phil, it's me, Shirley. Open your eyes, answer me. The old man had seemed asleep. Her voice turned wormy with insinuation: You want a chicken sandwich? Though his eyes remained closed he turned toward her. She looked up, saw my astonishment, and nodded: There, what do you think of that? I shook my head in disbelief. She took a sandwich from her knitting bag, which he ate right out of her hand while flat on his back with his eyes shut.

"Should I get her?" I asked as the man continued yelling.

"She hears him." My mother sounded uncharacteristically harsh. "Come on, we have to go."

We said good-bye to my father and left, but out in the corridor it was obvious that something was wrong, so I stopped, asked, waited.

My mother was struggling to answer. "There's something you should know," she finally said. "After I left yesterday Silverman and Dad had a long talk."

"Really?"

She nodded.

"About what?"

"Dad decided he'll take chemotherapy."

Immediately attuned to the somber, halting pace of this conversation I was caught unprepared when my mother started calling and waving. A man had stepped from a room three or four doors down.

"Dr. Bloom, excuse me, Dr. Bloom."

She started for him, leaving me to hurry after her.

This doctor wasn't dressed like a doctor. Short, stocky, in plaid pants and a short-sleeve shirt, he had wire-rimmed glasses on. The only concession to a uniform was the stethoscope around his neck.

"Do you have any news?" my mother asked after introducing us.

"Not a whole lot. The x-rays came back. I'm going to remove some fluid from your husband's chest. The way it is right now he's only getting partial benefit of his lungs."

"Is that much of a procedure?" I asked.

"No." He shook my hand again. "Alan," he said, "I'm very pleased to have you here. You'll be good medicine for your father."

"Did Dad talk about chemotherapy during the time he was home?" I asked in the elevator.

"No, and that was probably for the best. This way it was his decision, period."

"You don't think Silverman pressured him into it?"

She shook her head. "They already did the bone marrow last night."

"What's the next step?" She didn't know. In fact we were now on our way to Silverman's office; perhaps we'd learn something, but the secretary said Silverman had already left for the day. We climbed the basement stairs and tried to turn to other matters.

"Everyone keeps asking for you," my mother said.

The lobby was air-conditioned but outside the air was deadly, the kind that in times past might have signaled plague and quarantine, that nowadays you could do little more than drag yourself about in. When we were halfway across the boulevard the light changed, leaving us stranded on a four-inch-high, two-foot-wide median strip. Cars in the outer lane zoomed along as if on a speedway. Utterly vulnerable, standing directly in the path of any middle-aged driver's coronary, we were following the unmarked path that almost every white person who left the hospital followed, the path that led to East Flatbush, but at some point the ghetto would cross this boulevard and when it did my mother would have to move. Stop that, I told myself. One thing at a time.

"We have the light, let's go."

"Alan, I hate to mention this but there's a problem. I'm expecting the plumber sometime tomorrow. They don't tell you exactly when so do you think one of us should stay home and wait for him?"

"Sure. Of course."

I asked my father to lean forward then I put my hand behind his head and fluffed the pillow.

"They drained two bottles of fluid out of my chest while you were home."

"Was it painful?"

"Not too bad. It's when I go down for x-rays, that's where they get you. That x-ray table's hard as a goddamn rock."

I plunged in. "Mom told me you decided to take chemotherapy."

"Look, what could I do? This way there's just steady deterioration."

"You ought to do whatever you think's best, Dad."

"No matter what it's a losing proposition." His voice trailed off, then picked up. "The doctor wanted this."

"It's hard to believe you're worried about pleasing doctors. Don't *you* feel it's worth a try?"

He laughed. "I'm almost seventy-three years old. That's not the time to start fooling yourself. Three score and ten, am I right? Isn't that what it says in the Bible? Anytime you do better than that you're coming out ahead of the game."

I nodded.

"Right after the ulcer operation I thought maybe I'd have a couple more good years. It wasn't in the cards, that's all. Look, I can remember when anytime someone you knew went into the hospital you made it your business to say good-bye because chances were pretty good you'd never see them again, and that's no exaggeration."

"That's no exaggeration?"

"I'll put it this way. The only person I ever knew who was a patient in Mount Sinai Hospital up in the Bronx and lived to tell about it was my mother."

"Dad, what are you talking about? Do you hear what you're saying?" This sort of thing could drive me crazy.

"I'll tell you something else. The only reason she made it was all she had wrong with her was a bad tooth so how much damage could they do, but that's not what I'm talking about. I'm talking about serious illness, not petty stuff."

I saw the change in expression as he turned to the past and I cringed. "Rest awhile, Dad, okay? Don't talk so much."

You told me that a hundred times, I'd say. He'd turn away and sink yet more deeply into his chair, a Morris chair that accommodated itself to any posture, any person, particularly my father who, with a flawed diamond ring on his pinky, had been rejected several times by the New York police force in the 1920s when the minimum weight was 140 pounds because at five feet nine he'd never gotten over 135. Nevertheless the middle-aged potbelly had been predictable even then, inevitable, a consequence of poor stance. Working for the post office was pure chance: the job had been there, he didn't take it seriously, he thought of it as temporary, at least until the Depression, marriage and anyone with a steady income as well off: buying a car, a house, a washing machine; I was born, the war began and people who'd been in business for years and barely hanging on started making money, good money: the first heart attack! Sinking yet more deeply with his legs resting on the ottoman in front of the chair he'd go over the bets he was placing on the fights at Ridgewood Grove or the Garden, or he'd lean over and take a newspaper from the ottoman, anything to get something between us. Of course sometimes he'd do neither. Sometimes he'd answer me. Because those were very good days for me, he'd say. I know. You could buy a corned beef sandwich for a dime and cigarettes were ten cents a pack. Gyp the Blood was your pal and the *News* cost a penny. Dad, that was forty, fifty years ago. Why do you dwell on the past? Can't you enjoy yourself now? Now, formulating my own past, being unreasonable about it, being irrational, being stupid at his bedside I cringed staring at his arms folded on his chest, avoiding his face going from the dough-white skin of the inner wrist to the top of the other hand, his right hand where a cloverleaf of veins was speckled purple and gray with occasional black knots: small, soft bones no longer embedded in flesh, now plainly visible on a hand that could no longer hurt a fly, that could only hurt itself; this hand, as I stared at it, a memory, a rebuke, unexpectedly, unimaginably fragile.

"Coming home puts a crimp into your plans, doesn't it?" he said.

"No problem." We looked directly at each other until I turned away. "There's plenty to do around the house. Mom says you had a flood in the basement last week."

"Right."

"Maybe I'll get ambitious and reupholster those chairs in the breakfast room. Mother bought some plastic material and a staple gun. It shouldn't be too hard."

"How are your hemorrhoids?" Then he went on. "Oh, listen, Alan, remind Mother there's supposed to be a cost-of-living increase in the next pension check. It's not much but whatever it is it's better than nothing."

"I probably should get going, Dad."

"Before you go see if my slippers are near the bed." He made a motion as if to lean over and check but then didn't follow through on it.

The cement flowerpots that stood like turrets at either end of the porch ledge had held the power to excite, the power to enchant my childhood imagination. The porch had been a garden back then; begonias, geraniums, and petunias more colorful than my best marbles grew in these flowerpots. The porch had been a fort; I would duck behind the flowerpots and be protected from people on the sidewalk as I engaged in daring, imaginary adventures of every sort.

"How's your father?"

A white-haired man, a fairly new neighbor who until now I'd only nodded at, had crossed the street; he looked up at me as his dog pulled against the leash.

I told him in general terms.

He shook his head. "Damn shame."

The dog was pulling him away. I sat back, a victim of my own talents. Twenty minutes earlier I'd returned from the hospital.

"Dad just called," my mother said when I first walked in, and I froze. "Nothing's wrong, don't worry. He just wanted to say good night. Alan, your being here is good for Dad. I'm very pleased the two of you can talk. I can't tell you—."

"Okay, good," I said, cutting her short, repeating to myself: I need her reserve, period, nothing else, no gratitude. "I'm going out on the porch." And I was still on the porch, berating myself. All she'd wanted was to talk about the comfort I was bringing to her dying husband. Nothing was wrong with that but this: I was here as beneficiary—gaining experience, experiencing loss. Heartache and sorrow create lines; that opens doors. Stop it. That's ugly. He's dying. You're his son. Don't twist the whole thing out of shape.

"Mom, I'm coming in," I called. "You want me to leave the chairs out?"

"No. And lock up."

I stopped in the kitchen but she was standing at the stove stirring something as if that required total concentration.

"Dad's really mellowed," I finally said, "hasn't he?"

Slowly she turned and looked at me.

"Now he's mellowed?" she said. "I see. Wouldn't you say it's a little late for that?"

For a moment I remained where I was, then I was closing the bathroom door, taking a deep breath. The bleakness was like pain; perhaps it was grief; it was inexpressible. Standing over the basin brushing my teeth I looked in the mirror and saw my eyes begin to fill with tears. Watching the face crack, as a sob formed, I turned the faucet up to drown the sound. I looked ridiculous, just ridiculous, not grief stricken. In fact, with white runny toothpaste smeared on my lips I saw, as I looked into the mirror, what appeared to me to be the face of a clown.

———

The next morning my father called only moments before the sidebell rang: it was the plumber. My mother, relieved that he was here this early, went downstairs with him.

My father complained that he'd slept poorly.

"Was breakfast any good?"

"Not too bad."

We talked a bit before saying good-bye then I too went downstairs, where I found my mother in a quandry.

"He says we should put a cap on the drain," my mother said.

Standing at her side the plumber was expressionless.

"What's the alternative?" I asked.

"I'll be honest with you. You don't put a cap on, then you got yourself some job." The plumber opened the basement door and pointed to blackened chips of red brick scattered around the rim of the drain at the foot of the basement steps. "I pulled all this out just by sticking my hand down there. Drains have foundations you know. People don't realize this but a foundation's like anything else, when it gets old it'll fall apart and right now this one's starting to go."

Consequently he wanted the basement drain capped, explaining: "That way when the drain on the landing gets clogged, which it'll do the next time we get a storm, you got the drain up there in the middle of your backyard to take the backup. Just like I was telling your mother, if it overflows in the backyard so what, all that happens is it runs down the alley and into the gutter. No problem. You got the sewer at the corner, right. Let the city worry."

Is that legal, I wondered.

"That's fine except I don't know if I like the idea of the backyard flooding," my mother said.

"But this isn't the time for us to get started on some kind of big repair job, is it?"

Upstairs again I said, "Under the circumstances it's the best we could do." She seemed distracted. "From what Dad said I think he ate a good breakfast." This drew no reaction. "Mom, look, if capping the drain really bothers you that much—."

"It's not that, Alan. I was hoping when they took the fluid off Dad's chest the raspiness would clear up, but I still heard it over the phone."

"What's that mean, that the congestion is still there, is that it?"

"I'm afraid it's something else. You know what," she said, making up her mind, "I think we should go see Silverman right now."

It was a bit after 9 A.M..

As if it were a sanctified place, my mother and I spoke very quietly as we waited for him in his office. The hope was that after seeing Silverman we'd be able to track down and talk to a Dr. William Hill. It would be this Dr. Hill, evidently, not Davidson, who would administer chemotherapy. Davidson was no longer a member of the staff.

"Another thing. If Hazel comes today," my mother said, "I think we should give her a lift home. Why should she shlep on the bus?"

The door opened and Silverman greeted us—almost warmly. It was almost as if he were looking forward to this. There was something confident or relaxed about him as he tilted back in his swivel chair. Smiling, he appeared content to wait for one of us to begin.

"I guess we're at a new stage," my mother said, "is that right?"

He agreed things were definitely changing. "Mrs. Ware, whether you know it or not Dave's been pretty fortunate so far." He gave us time to reflect on that. "I'm sure you know that he's decided to try chemotherapy."

"And you think that's the right decision?" my mother asked. "After all, we're relying on your judgment."

"I don't see how he could have made any other decision."

I started to ask about time but Silverman didn't let me finish the question.

"Look, you have to understand something," he said. "I can't say how long Dave will live *without* chemotherapy, and I can't guarantee chemotherapy will be successful, so how could I possibly answer a question like that?"

"I'm sure you explained this before," my mother said, "but tell me again. What would you consider successful?"

"Mrs. Ware, I want to be supportive but I have to be realistic with you. At best chemotherapy can't do more than shrink a tumor."

"There's just one tumor?"

"The condition's spread, I think you know that." As if he were considering something he turned away from us toward a vacant corner of the room. "Maybe I should tell you this," he said, turning back. "When Dave agreed to chemotherapy he told me something else. I'm going to tell you exactly what he said. These are Dave's words: I hope my wife understands."

I felt myself flush. Those words were being used against us. He was quoting my father to put us in our place. Ironically the opposite happened. When he said that something clicked and suddenly I had an angle on my father's change of mind, or heart. My mother wasn't saying anything. Common sense dictated that I be conciliatory.

"Dr. Silverman, my mother and I never had any interest in making decisions for my father. He's decided on a course of action and as far as we're concerned that's the way it should be."

"Good. Alan, you saw your father yesterday, right? If he could stay the way he is things wouldn't be too bad but I'm going to be frank with both of you. Right now we don't have any idea how much pain and suffering he might have to go through in whatever time he has left."

As if punishment were being administered I sat stiffly, almost rigidly.

"If we can shrink the tumor, that's going to make it a lot easier for your father to breathe. It will make it easier for him to eat. Chemotherapy could eliminate at least some part of the suffering that might lie in store for your father."

"They took fluid off Dave's lungs last night," my mother said, "but when I spoke to him this morning he was still raspy."

"We can't get it all off, Mrs. Ware, and it's going to come back *again*, too. Dave's a very, very sick man."

"And when it comes back again, then what?"

Silverman sighed in frustration and turned to me.

"Dr. Silverman, there's only one thing about all this that bothers me. After the tumor shrinks won't it grow back again and then won't Dad have the very suffering you say you're going to alleviate?"

He stared at me. "What do you want me to do, Alan? Do you want me to kill him? We're trying to prolong this man's life. Why is that so difficult for you people to understand?"

Without giving a thought to consequences I said with absolute conviction although as it turned out not with absolute accuracy, in the sense that my statement was incomplete, "Dr. Silverman, why is it so difficult for you to understand that my father felt that agreeing to chemotherapy was a condition of returning to the hospital?" Even as I said, "Don't you know that?" I was looking for a way to back off. Ethical considerations. I didn't want to misrepresent. "I don't mean that he told me that, that's just what I surmised."

"I disagree. I disagree completely. He came back because he thought treatments would help. He knows that's all we can do for him."

What he went on to say was lost on me. I heard my mother; her words were spoken slowly, distinctly, as words will be when one is trying to restrain oneself. She was standing: "Thank you for your time, Dr. Silverman."

It wasn't until we reached the lobby that either one of us spoke.

"That bastard. Do we want to kill Dad: incredible. Can you imagine a doctor *saying* that."

I was on the living room couch. With the anger that had propped up my outrage now spent, I put a question to myself: Where in the hell did Alan Ware of all people come off harboring outrage? What in the hell had been the matter with me? Shed of anger my outrage seemed quaint, something to be placed under glass and exhibited in a museum but not in a doctor's office, not when I didn't have a goddamn thing to back it up with, no pull, no power, no donations to withhold, not even ties to minor figures in the underworld. Like insubordination, like the kind of sunburn that sent you to sick bay, my outrage might well have been considered a court martial offense. I'd undermined the purpose of our visit, which had been to gain information, and placed us in a mood that precluded flushing out Dr. William Hill.

Nevertheless it wasn't until I started into my father's room at two o'clock and saw that his bed was empty that I experienced an absolutely gut-wrenching sensation.

My mother was in the doorway. "See if he's in the bathroom."

I looked. "No."

At the nurse's station we were told my father had been scheduled for x-rays at 12:45.

If earth was a spaceship in a limitless universe, then Brooklyn was an elevator in a shaft without limits. After conferring briefly we decided I'd return to the room and my mother would go downstairs and try to find Dr. Hill.

As I entered 626 the elderly woman who was again seated at her husband's bedside caught my eye, waved me over, but before she had a chance to pump me for information an inhalation therapist came into the room; our attention shifted.

"Okay, Mr. Feeney, therapy, wake up."

There was no recognition on the part of the man in the middle bed. The therapist got him into an upright position, then placed an attachment over his mouth.

"Inhale. Deep, out, come on, Mike, cough, that's it, good."

After a minute or so he eased Mr. Feeney, whose protruding eyes remained open and expressionless, back down, then said good-bye and left.

"What's wrong with Feeney?" I asked.

"Poor circulation, plus he's senile like my husband." Our eyes drifted toward her husband who was lying on his back at the far edge of the bed with his face turned away from us. She spoke without prompting. "Blood clots on the brain." It was like an announcement. "Two years already he won't wake up."

"He talks," I said.

"Sure he talks, but he talks crazy. You didn't hear him? He talks against his children. By Phil his own children are murderers. Go do something."

"Your husband actually never opens his eyes?"

"Not for two years already. I should shout; that's what the doctors told me: when you talk to him shout." To illustrate she leaned forward, then put her mouth close to his ear: "Phil, this is Shirley. You want we should go home to Rego Park?" Her husband was completely unresponsive. Surprisingly, when she turned to me it wasn't pain or anguish but curiosity that I saw on her face. She was gesturing in the direction of the empty bed. "That's your father?"

"Yes. He's downstairs for x-rays right now."

"What's wrong?"

"He's a very sick man." That of course wasn't enough. "Very sick," I said. "Cancer."

"Ach. Gottenyu," she shuddered.

My mother returned to the room after discovering that Dr. Hill's office was located in the old section of the hospital. Still my father wasn't back.

An aide pushing a wheelchair came in. I didn't immediately connect the shriveled figure strapped into the wheelchair, being lifted out of the chair and placed in bed, with my father.

"There you go, Mr. Ware," the aide said, pulling the covers up to his chest.

After he'd gone my mother and I hovered over my father. Brown eyes glared out of dark sockets which were now sunk very deep in his head.

"Dad." His eyes met mine, lost focus, started to roll. "Dad." They refocused. "Do you hear me?"

He moved his eyelids.

"You want some water?" my mother asked.

He moved his lips.

"Shh. First take a sip." She held the glass close. "Good," my mother said, "that's it. That'll make you feel better." After a moment she took the glass away.

"We brought you some prune juice," I said.

"You should see what else we brought." My mother went to the chair for her handbag.

"You feeling any better?" I asked.

"A little water," he whispered.

My mother was holding up a pair of tiny scissors. "See. To cut your toenails."

A few minutes later he began to speak. "An hour I sat in that wheelchair. I said, Can't you please take me? When I finally got on the table they put me through some deal: hold your breath, breathe out—. I'm not up to that anymore."

"What the hell do they need all these x-rays for?" I said. Shaking my head I saw my aunt standing in the doorway. "Hazel." I immediately moved in her direction. "Mom said you might stop by. Look, you have a visitor, Dad."

He made the slightest nod, then closed his eyes.

When we were sure he was asleep I suggested they go to the lounge. "I'll stay here. Go ahead, go."

They returned a few minutes later accompanied by Florence and her husband, Harry. My father opened his eyes.

This was now an aging family.

Hazel, with a limp and a three-room apartment on Clinton Street, was unmarried; Hazel, on those infrequent occasions during my childhood when she stayed overnight with us, would go into the bathroom after the supper dishes were done and reappear an hour later in her housecoat and curlers just as drab and plain as ever yet changed in an eerie way: it was not the metal brace with the leather straps that was on her leg, or the shape of her nose or mouth; rather, like living room furniture that certain housewives keep under a sheet of clear plastic, her entire face, under a transparent layer of cream and lotion, would have taken on a moist, artificial shine. I'd try to avoid looking at her. The difficult lonely life she'd led hadn't deepened so much as hardened her. Self-supporting—a secretary—she was impatient of welfare and used words like *do-gooder* and *bleeding heart*. These last years she'd traveled: twice to Israel, through Europe, through French Canada, to Acapulco, to California. She never complained, nor did Flo, the even-tempered, overweight middle sister. I saw her squinting through curling smoke, a cigarette hanging from her mouth as she debated which card to throw: a player of canasta, poker, mah-jongg, she worked crossword puzzles, knitted scarves and sweaters, and after years of living in Hempstead was more adept than Harry at driving in Brooklyn. Harry, who went for fresh fruit the way she went for sweets, wore moccasins and shopped in army-navy stores. His pastime was fishing; he was a swimmer; he was a walker who used the Hempstead Public Library's toilet as a destination; he planted a garden; he lay in a hammock; he barbecued with a chef's hat and hated the fact that over the years he'd put money into Series E government savings bonds.

"You had a nap. Good," my mother said. My father stared but didn't respond. "Maybe we'll give Dad a sponge bath. Then he'll be in the mood for company." She pointed toward the doorway where the relatives stood. "You have company, did you know that?"

He nodded soberly, without looking.

My aunts and uncles left to wait in the lounge.

"Let's see. I think everything we need should be here," my mother said, opening the regulation nightstand, taking out the metal basin.

As she filled it with warm water I drew the curtain and raised the bed. Despite this flurry of activity there was a kind of passivity, a lack of curiosity about him. My mother returned, unbuttoned his top, then started soaping his chest with a washcloth. I tried to anticipate her moves so that I wouldn't have to stand idly by.

"Can you raise your arm, Dad?"

He did. Staring at me he held the arm stiffly, in a position that was difficult to maintain, yet he made no move to change it. This wasn't passivity, he was without volition; there was something almost subservient here.

"Okay, you can put it down. Now the other one."

The hand that he returned to his chest moved, crawled over his skin and down his body, directing my eyes toward the growth immediately below his waist that my mother had mentioned but which I'd never seen. I wanted to jerk my head away or shut my eyes: it was half a tennis ball, the cap of an oversized mushroom, dingy white, a knob with skin stretching so tightly across it that it shone; his fingers glided up it, his palm covered it; he was palming it, moving his hand back and forth as if he were polishing it, all this accomplished at an unhurried pace, almost absently, as he stared into space.

"Alan, wash Dad's back." She gave me the washcloth. When I finished I joined her at the foot of the bed where, without first asking, she pulled his pajamas down to his ankles then took them off. Not a word out of him, not a word; he didn't even acknowledge it.

"Lift your knees, Dad."

Since the meat that normally covers a behind was completely gone, when he obeyed three or four inches of excess skin was revealed lying flat on the sheet directly under the thigh he'd just raised: this skin a wrinkled flap extending out from his buttock like a vestigial organ: how grotesque: x-rays? what for? Anyone could see it, anyone. He was gone, eliminated, it was over: let him alone.

My mother, raising his foot, worked the washcloth between his toes, then went higher, quickly, without fuss, eventually reaching his crotch. I stared, no longer pretending to be useful. Nothing mattered. He had removed himself; evidently we could do as we pleased.

"There," my mother said after we had fresh pajamas on him, "isn't that better?"

He nodded, almost as a child might, then tried turning on his side, winced, and drew back.

"Don't move, lay still," she said, "just rest."

"Christ," he said with more strength than he seemed to possess, "let them do something. You couldn't handle me at home, that's why I came back." He was looking directly at my mother whose only answer was to lay her hand on his forehead, make a connection, smile gently. My legs trembled at the desperation in his voice, the desperation that shattered illusions of removal but the trembling didn't show and I wouldn't crumble now just as I hadn't crumbled before schoolyard fist-fights; fights that started with words or shoves, that built for a morning and afternoon or for a couple of days during a week, fights where I'd finally walk to a spot with a group of friends alongside or trailing behind, where a circle would form, fights I'd had hours or days to think about, my mind had had time to work on me, Ware, the willful misbehaver who'd discovered that by fighting it was possible to beat back the trembling that I couldn't prevent. The first blows would be quelling, anesthetic. As for afterward, though this behavior perplexed and drained my mother and drove my father to dark silence, I had glory. Each limping step was a strut and swelling on the side of my face or over an eye was better than any beard I'd grow later on.

She was stroking his forehead again and again as if there was a cowlick there that needed constant brushing back. Unobtrusively I backed away from the bed and went to the lounge.

I returned to the room with Hazel and Flo and Harry

"Alan, pull over some chairs," my mother said.

"Not for me. I'll wait outside," Harry said.

Moments later I joined him in the corridor.

"Terrible. Just looking at your father was getting me sick."

"The change from yesterday to today is incredible," I said. "I don't see how they're going to give him treatments."

A nurse went into the room. Flo, who'd entered knowing the situation, came out slowly, the shock of confirmation plastered all over her face. I broke the silence.

"How's Tyler and Sheila and the kids?"

"Fine thanks. Mitchell has chicken pox."

"Who's home with him?"

"Sheila. Her hours are flexible."

"Good. Harry, you enjoying retirement?"

"If you stuck it up your ass you'd never miss it. You understand what I'm saying?"

"Pretty much."

"You see what's going on in that room," he said. "That tells you what's left to look forward to."

"Harry, please," Flo said, "not now."

Hazel and my mother came out.

"The nurse is taking blood," my mother said.

"I think we'll get going," Flo said. "If there's anything we can do let us know."

A minute later, in a kind of ritualistic gesture, they bunched in the doorway for another look but the nurse had drawn the curtain.

"We'll tell Dad you said good-bye," I said.

My father picked up during the last few minutes of our visit. Nevertheless, I drove home as I might have walked had I been forced to walk many blocks: mechanically, listlessly. Everything seemed pointless.

He called home at suppertime and although we spoke only briefly—I told him I'd be returning for the evening visit—his voice sounded firmer than it had anytime that day.

As a white child pulls at the skin on the far side of his eyes so that he might play the Oriental, so the skin covering the surface of my father's face seemed stretched, stretched to the point that an entire kind of a lifetime's markings—the lines, the creases, the wrinkles—were wiped out, and in their place, like the nylon stocking worn as a mask by the stickup man, there existed a waxen landscape of vacancy. Despite that, lying in bed with the transistor radio on his pillow, he appeared calm and alert. There had obviously been a continuation of the improvement begun late in the afternoon.

"Hi, Dad." I asked what he was listening to.

"Alan, sit down."

He shut off the radio, waited, then began to unbutton his pajama top. When the top was half-unbuttoned he tapped the fragile bonework of his chest.

"There's something in here."

Slowly, somberly I nodded.

"I didn't want to upset Mother when I spoke to you before but I can't use the phone anymore."

"You called—."

"The nurse had to dial it. I tried, Alan. No more. I can't even get out of bed anymore. There can't be much left."

"Dad, shh—."

"I'm sorry, Alan."

"What do you have to be sorry for?"

"I did okay."

"Sure you did. Of course you did."

"We have some money. Did you know that?"

I shook my head.

"I didn't either. Mother saved it up without telling me. It's going to be hard on Mother for awhile. Do what you can to help her."

I didn't trust myself to speak.

"I'm tired, Alan."

Involuntarily responding to a deep-seated enthusiasm for metaphor, I assumed he was talking about life, but evidently he wasn't; he fell asleep.

"I'm home."

My mother hurried from the bathroom. "How was Dad?"

I shrugged and cast my eyes downward.

"Oh," she said, "I see." There was a tinniness, a slightly shrill rise in her voice: disappointment.

That revealed hope.

It wasn't reasonable but she was still hoping, and not by way of some desperate last-minute faith either; rather, this hope was demanded by an internal force. Internally generated, a life force, it pushed her to the breaking point even as it held her back, even as it kept her going.

What did I know about such a state, such a position: how dark, at least I knew that. And the paradox: the closer his end drew, the more he shriveled, the more completely he was filling her world. Of course. Of course. But seeing it up close lent magnitude. To gather the fullness of this response I saw and I heard and I felt, was touched, chilled, made stupid by the absolutely incontrovertible: by finality, by conclusion. Soon all that would remain would be for her to be old, alone. Faced with that who wouldn't hope, who wouldn't tighten to bloodlessness, to tin in the voice.

"Mom, let's sit down." At the breakfast table with its two leaves stored underneath for all those times when company came, in this setting that reached back to my adolescence, that reached to my childhood, I told her exactly what the situation was: "Dad can't even dial the phone anymore. He can't even get out of bed." I repeated the entire conversation, and then I told her that he said that he was sorry.

"He's sorry? Believe me, *I'm* sorry."

"What he means is, he's sorry you're going through all this. He knows how hard this is on you."

"I understand. You don't have to explain it." I felt awkward, embarrassed. "Believe me, I know Dad cares." She paused: "An hour after one of our arguments was over Dad would be ready to put his arms around me. That's the way your father was."

"He did his best," I said.

"That's right. Look, we lived within our means and we always had enough. Not everyone can say that, and anyway what's the difference. By now it's ancient history," she said, as if she would push it aside and go onto something else but she couldn't and moments later there was some more. "I was the one who accepted the way things were, Dad was the one who couldn't. Once the war started his salary didn't stretch very far. People we knew, neighbors, ordinary working people right here on the block started raking it in. The one exception was government employees. I tried to tell Dad, look, this is the situation and either you learn to live with it or you make a change but Dad couldn't do that, instead he grumbled and he complained and he found fault and he criticized and everything in the past became wonderful, which it wasn't, and as far as the present was concerned no matter what it was he could take very little enjoyment in it. It was sad. Believe me, he wasn't really angry at the world; whether he knew it or not he was angry at himself."

I nodded my head in melancholy agreement.

"Alan, I can talk about Dad but that doesn't give me the courage to ask about you."

"Me?"

"You see my plans," she said. "I'm not thinking past the next day, but what's going to be with you?"

"You mean in terms of my personal life? I don't know what to say."

"Believe it or not, when you broke up with Carol"—she spaced her words—"Dad was very disappointed."

"No, I didn't know that. I knew he liked her but. . . ."

"It wasn't only that. Look, you're thirty-two. I think Dad felt"—she closed her eyes as if, no matter how painful, this had to be said—"he hoped you'd get married."

"Really?"

Looking at me steadily, shrugging, smiling apologetically as though this might sound silly and I should bear with it, she said, "Look, you're his son, we're still old-fashioned, he's concerned about you. He thought you'd have children, you'd have a family—that's important to us. Wait, let me finish. When a child sees his parents not getting along it's frightening, but I'm not sure you understood the other side. Dad did. Dad knew our marriage was the one thing he had that he could count on. He understood it was very good for him."

I was uncomfortable with this conversation and I wanted to turn it.

"Half the time Dad said things," I said to my mother, "I knew he was really just looking for an opportunity to get under people's skin. I knew there was never any real antagonism on his part and I'm sorry if it ever seemed that I didn't know that."

"I'm glad you see that you weren't faultless.

"Of course I wasn't."

"Dad wanted the two of you to be closer."

"I'm sure he did."

"I'll tell you something else. He was afraid you'd be like him."

"What makes you say that?"

She didn't answer, nor was there any need to.

"I don't know what to say, Mom."

"There's nothing to say. It's hard for a parent to give to a child when he thinks what he has isn't worth giving."

Though she would have disclaimed any knowledge of the grammar of revision, it was likely she was attempting just that. Though the revision was not convincing, the attempt was undermining me. I suffered a sudden attack of sentimentality but recovered quickly, stood up.

"Oh, I meant to tell you. I bumped into Dr. Bloom when I was leaving. He was very friendly."

"I see."

Toward morning a dream woke me. I was in a large public room which without being cold was devoid of warmth. Eyeglasses were piled in one corner; there was a pile of dentures next to it. Looking out through one of several dirty windows I saw barren ground enclosed by rows of barbed wire, and it was then that I realized this was a concentration camp. I walked through a door into a tunnel and came out in a barracks. Rows of cubicles twisted in front of and behind me. Emaciated, skeletal inmates were everywhere. Then, as I knew I would, I saw my father; he was huddled on the floor in striped prison pajamas holding a metal cup in trembling hands trying to drink. I backed away from him at the very time that I tried moving toward him, and woke up.

Though frightened my mind was clear and I tried to calm myself: that was a dream, you're in bed, it's over. There seemed to be no reason to be upset by the dream. That is, by coincidence, sheer coincidence, cancer patients often come to resemble concentration camp victims and I'd made the connection, but in fact the connection was purely visual.

He was a victim, yes, but no human being was victimizing him; dismiss the dream, go back to sleep. It was nearly morning.

But I couldn't sleep. In the classroom I was the one who gave highest ratings to the workings of the unconscious. How odd: my dream being so misguided, so off base.

On the other hand, perhaps the dream revealed the extent to which I felt wronged.

"Dry as could be," I said to my mother the following morning after checking the cellar. We'd had a storm during the night. It wasn't until after we'd eaten and showered and were having another cup of coffee that my mother gave in to the pressure.

"I'm going to call Dad."

The phone rang until I was sure it wasn't going to be answered and then, "Hello?"

"How are you?" she asked.

The voice was very weak. "No good."

"What's the matter?"

Last night, without ever hitting a false note, without ever stepping out of character, he made it clear that he was reconciled to dying. It might have been assumed that after he'd expressed his concern for us the final word had been spoken, that some natural force, some universal law of symmetry or design would see to it that he wouldn't alter his attitude or position, because to retreat now, to waffle in any way, would be anti-climactic, an indignity, and absolutely, utterly futile. Over and against that, the consequence of his position, despite the fact that it had been reached without taking into account whether or not it would please anyone, would have been life as art rather than vice versa, and to believe that that would come to pass required innocence of a stripe too unimaginable for me to conjure up. When the laws of probability, with the long stretch of history on their side, were in competition with the slim line of aesthetic principle, there could be little doubt which would prevail.

"At eight o'clock I was downstairs for x-rays. Silverman saw me and he told me they'll need more before they do anything."

"Jesus."

"I don't understand," he said. "Why don't they start?"

"Try not to aggravate yourself," my mother said. "You'll feel stronger in a little while."

"There's more."

"Not today though. The rest of the day you'll take it easy."

"Listen to me. A little while ago," he paused as if running out of breath, "Bloom came in. He had a release with him. What could I do?"

"What was it for?" I asked.

"He says they have to do a biopsy on my liver. I signed."

According to *Women's Wear Daily*, or Paris, or Seventh Avenue, slacks and pantsuits were now proper for women in almost any situation. My mother, who took full advantage of this change, had taken to saying, It's what they show today, but when the style had first appeared she'd been more forthright, admitting, This is the biggest break we could have gotten, referring to herself and all those women like her whose ankles and knees would swell from periodic flareups of arthritis, a condition many older women tolerated but, conscious of their appearance, hated to see exposed.

The bottom of my father's face had collapsed, in part because they'd removed his upper and lower plates. In a sort of inverted pucker his lips, it seemed, were being sucked down into his mouth. 2:20 P.M. Exactly twenty minutes after we arrived he returned from his second trip of the day to x-ray, this time in even worse shape, apparently, than he'd been the day before.

My mother's flared slacks were sharply creased. The light blue short-sleeve blouse she had on looked like a man's except for the exaggerated collar. We were standing at either side of my father's bed. It wasn't depth or strength but the narrow borders I'd assigned to reality that kept this moment from paralyzing me.

"I couldn't have made it back"—his voice was roughened air, not firm sound—"except they strapped me into the wheelchair."

"We were here when they brought you in. Shh—, don't talk."

"Alan, let's freshen Dad up."

We drew the curtains and inside the enclosure yesterday's procedure was today's routine. To insulate myself I handled my father as if he were so many separate pieces.

"Alan," he said, "get the urinal."

Reaching through the curtain I saw that aunts Hazel and Flo had again shown up.

"Oh, hi Mort." He was in the hall with Harry. "You just get here?"

"A few minutes ago. How's your father?"

"We just gave him a sponge bath so he's feeling a little better. I'll be back in a minute."

Dr. Bloom was in the doorway of one of the small offices at the rear of the nurse's station, operating, the sole of a raised foot flat against the doorjamb behind him, his arms extending straight out so that his hands rested against the doorjamb in front of him. The casual corkscrew of his body was a studied affair, and if the short redheaded nurse he was talking to were to step into the office she'd do so by going under the bridge formed by his extended arms. Though there may well have been differences between them, the posture they together formed was itself an arrangement, stating: We are engaging each other, we're flirting. In a bar, on the beach, almost anywhere, at a party in the hallway next to the hat tree and evidently here too yes of course, why should I be jolted, this was soap opera heaven, serial material, hell, Bloom was probably a well-known stud, for all I knew he had a pilot's license or wrestled Greco Roman in international competition.

"I'm sorry, Dr. Bloom," I said when he came over, "but could you please tell me what in the hell is going on? When they brought my father back from x-ray he was completely out of it."

"How's he now?"

"Not too good. Is he getting pain medication?"

"Some. Alan, look, we don't want to put him on too much medication too early. We'll need it later."

"Let me ask you something. Would pain killers interfere with the treatment he's supposed to get?"

"I doubt it, but to be totally honest I'm not sure. I suppose you know there's going to be a liver biopsy."

"That's why I'm here. I want to ask you about that."

"It shouldn't be too hard on him. I know this isn't easy advice to follow but try to bear in mind your father probably looks a good deal worse than he actually feels."

"When do you do the biopsy?"

"Probably tomorrow."

I walked into the room wondering if during my absence my father had said anything at all to my mother about the biopsy.

In the remaining hour of our visit he kept close watch on me, and on my mother too, the movement of his eyes corresponding to our movements. This became more obvious when the relatives were gone. He seemed to want to keep one of us always in sight. His expression was intent yet utterly without demand. It asked no question of us; indeed, it had a quieting effect, so much so that we stopped fussing over him. Not for a moment did he doze. When it came time to leave my mother bent and kissed him on the forehead. I touched his hand.

"Take a little nap."

"See you later, Dad."

"Okay, Alan."

As soon as we were in the hallway I asked, "Did Dad ever say anything about the biopsy?"

"No."

"Bloom thinks it'll be tomorrow. Dad never mentioned *anything* about it?"

"No. And I didn't have the heart to bring it up."

"It has to be on his mind," I said.

"I'm sure it is."

"I wish they wouldn't do that," my mother said. A handbill advertising aluminum siding was stuck in the grillwork of the screen door. "People can think no one's home when they see that. Who wants to give anyone ideas these days?"

I was unresponsive, yet moments after dropping off to sleep in the front room I found myself recoiling from a series of nightmarish images which had obviously been inspired by my father's situation. I made my way to the kitchen where I did what I could to help.

Supper was quiet.

"That was really nice of Mort to come over from Jersey. Who would have expected him to make a trip like that in the middle of a working day."

"You know the family, they don't stand on ceremony. At least we're lucky in that respect."

"Did he say how Shellie's feeling?"

"The same."

"Boy, talk about problems, that would be something to live with, wouldn't it?"

"I feel so bad about that, yet there's nothing any of us can do."

In anticipation of my appearance my father must have had his eyes trained on the doorway because he started speaking before I'd taken a full step into the room. Since I'd primed myself to come in upbeat I couldn't check my greeting just like that. "Hi, Dad, how you feeling?" I said, and in effect we canceled out each others' words. Nevertheless I heard that his voice was no longer infirm.

By the time I was at his bedside we were both silent. He stared up at me as if he were waiting for something or expecting something; then in a sudden violent movement he threw the covers off.

"Dad." Something was totally out of whack. He was arching his hips, starting to push the pajamas down from his waist. "Hey, what are you doing? Wait a—oh my God."

Completely exposed, a puddle of chocolate filled the seat of his pants, which were now down at his knees; his naked thighs and buttocks were marked by this same runny chocolate mess.

"Clean me. The lamp came out."

"Jesus."

"The store is spent," he said while watching me carefully, using the tone he'd use when explaining something. He was absolutely unselfconscious.

I wanted to plead, Please, Dad, you're not making sense. Stop talking like this. He'd propped himself up on his elbows.

"Clean me. Come on."

"I'm getting ready to. I'll get the basin."

He nodded, momentarily relaxing.

"Supper rained. I couldn't eat."

I walked around the bed drawing the curtain as I went. "It's in the nightstand. You see what I'm doing? I'm closing the curtain so people won't see in."

He was nodding.

"You didn't eat?" I bent down, got the basin. "Now I'll go into the bathroom and fill it up, okay?"

"Okay."

As the water ran I thought, I just found my father this way. I'm the only one who knows. This is incredible.

"See," I said as I walked from the bathroom to his bed. He watched me carefully. At the bed I bent down and placed the basin on the braces attached to the door of the nightstand. When I straightened up my father's hips were arched: he was pulling the bottoms back up to his waist.

It was as if I were witnessing an act of supernatural dimension. When he was through he had a look of satisfaction on his face.

Hesitantly I asked, "Is that better?"

He nodded.

"Can I dump the water out? Are we all through?"

"Sure. What's Hazel's name?"

"Hazel? My aunt? You mean your sister-in-law?"

He nodded.

"What's her name? That's what you're asking me?"

"Yeah."

"Her name's Hazel, Dad, Hazel Perlman."

"I know. What's her name?"

"Dad, I have to talk to the nurse a second. I'm going to open the curtain so you can look out into the hall, then I'll be back as soon as I can."

I half ran down the hall to the nurse's station.

"Nurse, my father, in room 626, Mr. Ware—something's happened."

She finished distributing the last few cards in the filing cabinet near her desk before looking up. The twin peaks of her nurse's cap, like the facade of a toy castle, topped a certain starched appearance.

"What is it?"

"I can't describe it exactly. When I walked in his words weren't making sense."

"He was a little confused this afternoon."

She knows. She was supposed to be surprised. I'd thought she'd run to the room with me.

"Confused? I was here three hours ago and he wasn't like this."

"He started calling for your mother when visiting ended. We had to remind him she was gone because that kind of behavior can get a whole floor upset."

"You're telling me that my father was yelling for my mother?"

"For a little while. Most of the time he's very cooperative but for a while, yes, he was."

I remained there. I had to gather myself. The nurse's fortyish face was without makeup, or blemishes, or beauty.

"He's dirty. Could you please have him cleaned. He had a bowel movement in bed."

"I'll send someone down."

"Alan, this is the biggest, the most, most—."

"Take your time."

"Did you get the doors?"

"What doors, Dad?"

"No. Did you get the *doors?* Did you?" He smacked his hand down on the bed as if he were thoroughly disgusted then turned his face away. He turned right back. "Alan?"

"What Dad?"

"Give me the spill. Come on, I need the spill."

"The spill?"

"Yeah."

"I don't know what the spill is."

He rolled his eyes in exasperation.

"Do you mean this?" I pointed to the radio on the table. "Is this what you want?"

"The spill. The spill. Are you here?"

"Yes, Dad, yes."

"Where's Mother?"

"She's not here. Mother doesn't come at night."

"She doesn't?"

"No. Not for a long time." I sat down at the side of the bed and stared at the floor. "She didn't come at night the last time you were in the hospital either."

"I'm very surprised at that," he said.

"You told her not to, don't you remember?"

"I'm in bad shape, Alan. I want to talk to Mother."

"You know you're in bad shape?"

He nodded.

"Do you have any pain?"

"Okay, just give me the pill."

"What pill?"

"The pill goddamn it, the pill." He was pointing to the top of the nightstand.

"There's no pill there."

He was very agitated. "What about yesterday?"

"Do you mean this?" I picked up the package of hard candy that we'd bought. He shook his head. "Is this what you want?" I showed him the tissues.

"No."

"This?" I pointed to the phone.

He nodded. I held it in front of him and, concentrating, squinting, he brushed a fingertip over the dial a few times, then looked up at me.

"Were you trying to call Mom?"

He nodded.

I put the phone back on the nightstand. "That's not a good idea. She's not home. She went over to Anna's for a little while."

The agitation vanished; suddenly he appeared vulnerable and innocent and he said in a subdued voice, "I'm surprised at that." He looked away. Then the door opened. He turned back calling, "Rose, Rose," but of course it wasn't my mother; it was an orderly holding a pair of rubber gloves.

Looking first at my father and then to me he said, "Nurse told me someone in 626 shit in bed. Who did it, him?"

I drove at a snail's pace. How, I was wondering, could I break this news? Turning onto Forty-sixth Street I was confronted by a gutter cluttered with kids who, in a display of impudence, ignored my approach. I came to a complete stop; then they cleared a path which, when I started to move, turned into a gauntlet. They slapped the car's trunk, pounded the fenders, yelled, Get a fucking horse and You going to take all day?

I didn't know how to handle it. After pulling the car up the alley and into the garage I walked into the house.

"I'm in here, Alan." My mother was sitting on the living room sofa, stretching. "I guess I dozed."

"I have something to tell you."

"What's wrong?"

"Don't jump. Dad's the same. He might even be stronger. Physically."

"Physically?"

It took some moments before I could bring myself to say: "His mind. . . ."

Her eyes grew large; she whispered, "Could you have been mistaken?"

"No."

"My God," she said as I told her, "my God."

I had a question: why now? Was it coincidence that his mind had snapped when the liver biopsy was coming up? Was it physiological, psychological, self-induced, an escape?

"From here on out it's going to be very hard on us," I said some minutes later, "but for Dad the worst is over. He's gone."

"I never would have believed this. Can you imagine such a thing happening to your father? Never, never in my *wildest* dreams could I have imagined this."

"I know, Mom, I know." Though not above giving voice to the urge to lay blame or accuse, I felt myself about to express legitimate concern. "Mom, I hate to say it but do you think they might go ahead with the biopsy anyhow?"

Certain bureaucratic foul-ups are classic, reassuring. They confirm our most basic view of things yet they're upbeat: a grandmother receives notice to report for the draft; a bus driver is sent a $150,000 tax refund. Such nonsense makes the news and leads to a smile. There are other equally classic foul-ups: form letters are sent which threaten the loss of gas or electric if you don't pay up when in fact there is no unpaid balance, nor anyway of getting someone in authority to straighten out the matter; operating on the wrong patient; amputating the wrong leg.

Had the biopsy been canceled?

"How'd you sleep, Mom?"

"So so."

"Same with me."

We arrived at the hospital at 8 A.M. Normal considerations—weather, events of the day—were absent. No one was challenging our right to be here, not the guard in the lobby, not the gray-haired black man operating the elevator. As we started down the sixth-floor corridor common sense told me to walk in front of my mother so that I'd be the one to enter first.

"Get me the pill," my father said the moment I appeared in the doorway. The tone was forceful, demanding, but certain changes belied this force, declared his diminution; rather than his own pajamas he was now in a white hospital gown; the bedrails had been raised.

Still in the doorway my mother delicately, almost tremulously, raised her right hand and touched her fingertips to her lips.

"Are you all right, Mom?"

"Yes," she said.

"Get me the pill," my father said.

"You're sure you're okay?"

"Alan, I'm all right."

I attended to my father, walked to the nightstand, lifted the phone.

"No."

"No?"

He smacked an open palm on the bed, then acknowledged my mother for the first time. "Will you please give me the pill?"

She asked softly, "Can I give it to you?"

He nodded yes.

I was mystified.

My mother pointed to the nightstand. "Is it here?"

"I don't get it," he said. "What the hell's the big deal?"

She reached for the package of Charms. "No," he said. She picked up a cup. "No." The next item was a pencil. "Okay," he said, but when she went to hand it to him he laughed in ridicule.

"This *isn't* what you want?" she asked.

His expression, which was childlike in its exaggeration, reflected utter and absolute dismay. He looked to the ceiling for help.

All that was left on the nightstand was a pad. "Do you want a piece of paper, Dad?"

"Should we write something down?" My mother was speaking as if to herself. "The phone. Dave," she said, "do you want our telephone number at home, is that it? Did you forget what it is?"

He was nodding.

We exchanged looks as she wrote it out.

"There, see. Now I'll put it in the drawer so it won't get lost."

"That's right," he said, relaxing, satisfied.

After taking care of one or two housekeeping chores, changing him, having his bedding changed, with things more or less under control, we went to see Silverman.

Though for me the drama of the last days had reached its climax the night before, it had taken my mother's presence to conclude or round out this aspect of the drama. Seeing things in those terms made me self-conscious; my choice of terms opened the door to anti-climax. Was I really that much of a hothouse flower? Wouldn't it be curious if art turned out to be one of the more dehumanizing of specializations? Could anyone imagine an ordinary working person experiencing the conclusion of his father's life as, of all things, anti-climactic?

And it didn't stop at that. When meeting Dr. Hill a day or so later I quickly saw how flawed my preconception of the man was. It was simplistic, especially in contrast to the need I felt to give depth and dimension to characters I created for the page. I was mulling this confusion, this perversity, over even as Hill was saying to my mother, "Your husband can withstand a brain scan, otherwise I wouldn't go along with it. But let me say this. I'd never proceed except in consultation with Dr. Silverman. Your husband is Dr. Silverman's patient."

Anyway, anti-climax didn't turn out to be a problem, perhaps because my internal clock somehow malfunctioned.

Discovery of my father's shattered mind took something out of us. From the point of that discovery on we were in a sense played out. Silverman flatly refused to rule the liver biopsy out, and we backed down. He said my father's mental condition, if caused by new calcium formations or dehydration, might be reversible. Now the first order of business was a brain scan; that was what he told us. Shortly after that, when Bloom found us in my father's room, I told him I couldn't understand Silverman's position.

"Tests. Why more tests at this point?"

He looked uneasy, evaded the question, said that he wanted to remove fluid from my father's chest later in the afternoon or in the evening.

"It's no real discomfort, I give you my word."

"You mean you want me to sign," my mother said.

"Yes." He had two releases with him. "I also want to do a spinal tap."

My father couldn't sign for anything; even Silverman agreed he could no longer give informed consent.

When we were alone my mother said, "I'll probably sign anything they want. I can't fight them."

"I know," I said, and it was that discouragement, that resignation that defined the way in which we were played out.

During the last few days of my father's life I experienced time as I never had before. I lost my sense of it. Even with three meals a day to keep me on schedule I had no sense of continuity: I'd be in the hospital, then in a doctor's office, then home: always without apparent transition.

People—certain experts—say time may be incremental. There may exist some basic unit, some particle which is absolutely indivisible, irreducible. During that period I had the feeling they were probably onto something.

Hand in hand with that splintering came a change in my personality, in sensibilities. Normally some understanding of my sensibilities could be had by knowing I believed there was occasional genuine profound personal loss in almost every adult life. Of course I could imagine a life in which loss was absent, in which events of a destructive nature somehow didn't occur; I could even allow for love in that life and for early and deserved success which would last into and through middle age, but I believed that even in that lucky life—particularly in that lucky life—a strange sad change would occur; that lucky person would harden. That was my view. Yet I softened, became, during those final days, a kind of vulgarized or popularized version of myself.

I was often at his bedside. After he'd been placed on IV, as his head turned from one side of the pillow to the other, and back, I thought, Things don't turn out for the best, you have to make the best of things. And near the very end, as he lay in bed, his eyes unseeing, not yet flat and unlighted as in death, but rigidly fixed in an unfocused glare, as I tried to resist a sudden, strongly felt impulse, I thought, The real coward is the person who's afraid of himself.

Homiletic, platitudinous, with a whiff of broad appeal, these thoughts didn't bear my stamp; they suggested a sensibility more patently commercial than I took my own to be.

As I went through changes so did my mother. My father's gray slacks had been draped over the back of the chair that stood next to the nightstand on his side of their double bed ever since my return. I didn't feel I could say anything but I wished she'd hang them up in the closet. She couldn't bring herself to clear the top of the dresser either, to put away the key ring, the deck of cards, his wristwatch, all casually deposited, it seemed, just before going to bed.

Leaving things as he'd left them could become theater, the theater of piety, flaunting, flagrant, and sanctimonious. It was not her way. In fact she was undergoing a process of divestiture, a process of physical and psychological divestiture that would take strength to survive. She was thinner now, sharper, often silent. Ironically, this reduction of social surfaces created the appearance of stoic acceptance.

Events overtook strategies, if in fact any medical strategies actually existed.

"I need a skill."

"A skill. Can you show me what that is?"

He answered quietly. "I want to die."

I watched someone in a lab coat try to hit a vein in my father's arm: five times, six times. . . . Saliva dripped from the corner of his mouth. I walked away.

"There should be *such* a change in a person in a couple of days," the old lady, Mrs. Rothstein, said.

I asked about her husband.

"Moscowitz wants to put him in a Home. That's the new idea, so we'll see."

"The sill," my father said.

By the time I reached the bedpan it was too late. I located a nurse who called an orderly; they drew the curtain and a few minutes later the bedding had been changed and a rectal tube inserted.

"This morning your father was telling me he's thirty-four years old," the nurse said.

"Oh yeah?"

She stood looking at him with affection, then said, "Well, I'll see about some medication."

"Where's Mother?"

"In the lounge with Lou. You've been sleeping."

Lou was short and portly, a successful businessman with bushy eyebrows and brown eyes. The puffiness under those eyes, which was beyond the claim of a good night's sleep, which no vacation could ever again make vanish, suggested that he was somehow paying for his decency, for his generosity, for being the person that family and friends had long depended on.

In business success had come early. Still based in Brooklyn but linked by contract and contribution to shakers and movers not only in Washington but even in cities like Tampa and New Orleans, he and Ceil, soon after marrying, had settled in a residential section of the borough that offered direct access to the beach, that was exclusive enough to have competed with the finest suburbs for the attention of burglars going back to the 1940s.

He approached the bed cautiously, as if the person in there might be asleep. Then, without intending to, he turned back and looked at my mother and I again saw what he was seeing for the first time: a face made desolate, with all its particularizing characteristics obliterated. Just as my father's past had been eliminated from his face, so did this face advertise his future.

"So this is how you're spending your time," Lou said. He was gripping the raised sidebars.

"I did okay. Good-bye Lou."

"Good-bye? Come on, don't talk like that. That's no way to talk."

Flustered, protective of my uncle, my mother said, "Listen to me. I'm your wife, you always listen to me, don't you? You'll be here for your eightieth," my mother said, but my father wasn't listening.

"Rose, a skill."

"That means medication," I said. "Not yet, Dad, it's not time. I'll ask the nurse in a couple of minutes."

"Where's the pill?" he said.

"Just where it always is Dad, in the drawer."

"Show Dad," my mother said, "he wants to see."

I went to the nightstand, took out the slip of paper with our telephone number on it, and put it in his hand.

I was at a loss a few minutes later as I walked Lou to the elevator. He took a handkerchief from his pocket. "Why do they have to suffer like that?"

Though he couldn't provide it, when problems cropped up and help was needed, people, perhaps out of habit, still turned to him, and he responded with concern. Not his experience, not his cash or connections could unclog their arteries, though, or clean out their cancers or stay their strokes, which meant in effect that more and more often these days this uncle was enlisted in other people's lost causes.

"Look," he said, sighing, as we stood apart from the others while waiting for the elevator, "give your mother all the support you can. I don't know what else to tell you."

"I know. There's just not too much to say."

It was not his sleep which kept us silent, but, as it was with persons on a vigil, conversation would have been inappropriate, intrusive. His irregular breathing was scratchy, like static, as unmistakable in meaning as the whistle of an artillery shell or the report of a weapon.

"Are you waking up?"

My mother bent over and touched her lips to his cheek.

"Hi, Dad. How do you feel?"

He nodded, tried turning toward the bedside table.

"What are you looking for?"

"The spill."

My mother lifted the sheet and showed my father that the urinal was already between his legs.

The pain was beginning to make itself felt. I thought of going to the nurse's station to see if it was time for his medication.

He began moving his head back and forth as if in a bad dream. "Oh God," he said, "oh God."

I asked my mother to ask the nurse about medication, then I bent close to my father.

"Dad, do you hear me?"

He nodded.

"Do you hear me?" By opening and closing an eye, an eye which conveyed awareness, an awareness that I feared was about to fade out, he let me know we were still in contact.

"Can you still hear me?" I asked, trying to hold him there.

"Help me. Oh, please. Please. Please."

"Dad."

"Please. Please." His voice was growing louder. "Please, please, police. Police. Police," he yelled as my mother returned with the nurse.

"Do you think this can go on much longer?" I asked.

The drama of the last days had reached its climax but tension continued to build, tension of a different nature. There was a shift. As he lay in bed, his eyes unseeing, fixed in that rigidly unfocused glare, I wondered at my impulse, understanding that action based upon such impulse would constitute a violation, would be, beyond question, taboo.

"Dad." There of course was no response.

What was it that allowed me to stand, close the door, approach his bed, draw the curtain. Inside the enclosure I checked for seams of light. None.

I bent over the bedrail, raised my hand, then in a move so swift that it surprised me, my palm shot out toward his face, stopped, of course, with inches to spare. He didn't even flinch.

I felt mechanical, robot-like, though my arms and legs trembled and my hot neck itched as if I were wearing wool, and I had no idea how to undo what I'd just done, what, like a bedwetter in the midst of wetting, I was still, despite myself, doing: passing my hand back and forth, back and forth in front of his eyes, testing, not that I could see, I couldn't. Shapes floated in front of me, black and white worms and dots and little boomerangs, the sort of shapes I used to see under my high school microscope and what if someone walked in, my God, a nurse. I whirled at the thought but it was no one. All there was was the blue curtain hanging in folds from the silver runners on the ceiling.

Then somehow I was back in the orange plastic chair: I had to catch my breath. It was as if I'd dropped from a considerable altitude at a much too rapid rate. I needed time, I needed to let my very blood catch up to me.

"Bloom said the x-rays didn't show any shadow, or maybe it was mostly shadow. Anyway, it looks like his lungs are filling up with fluid again."

The family was seated in a corner of the lounge. They stared off into space as I spoke, or nodded slowly, without expression.

"He's only getting 200 calories from the IV and they can only give him three bottles a day, so the next thing they'll do is put a tube in his nose and he'll be able to get 2,000 calories that way."

"Nurse, I'm sorry to bother you again but can't you give him something? He's really in terrible pain."

"He's getting codeine every four hours."

"I know, but it's very bad for him right now."

"It's early. I'll be down as soon as I can."

"Okay. Thanks."

There was no recognition.

"Please. Help me. Please. Police. Police. Kill it."

"What's he saying? I couldn't make it out."

"Nothing. Just words. He's totally out of it, Harry."

I reached the kitchen just as my mother was hanging up the phone.

"That was the hospital. Dad's on the critical list."

Neither one of us knew how that worked, what line had been crossed.

At the main desk we found out we were no longer restricted to the normal visiting hours, now we could be here twenty-four hours a day. He seemed very far from consciousness. "Being placed on the critical list must just be some kind of formality," I said. His breathing was rhythmic now, and noisy. Though in those respects it mimicked snoring, this breathing would never be confused with that, nor was previous exposure to a death rattle necessary to know that harsh, fragmented sound which marked each inhale and exhale was just exactly that.

A luncheonette without a name was located between a liquor store and a laundromat.

When we returned a nurse and two doctors we'd never seen before were gathered at my father's bed.

"Could you wait outside please?"

While standing in the hall I saw Bloom approaching. I separated myself from my mother, spoke to him alone.

"The hospital called this morning and said Dad's on the critical list."

He nodded.

"How close is it?"

"I can't tell you that, but if there's family out of town I think you could prepare them."

There were flurries of activity all through the day.

Relatives came.

"No one wants to say anything to us," I said.

Nothing seemed to change.

"Who knows how long it could go on like this, Mom."

The phone rang later than anyone in the family would call. My mother was in the bathroom. I was watching the late news. I ran to answer it then stood as she drew near.

"Should I take it?" I asked.

"All right."

"Hello."

"Rose Ware, please. This is Belmont Hospital calling." It was a neutral female voice.

"I'm her son. She asked me to take any messages."

"Could you please ask Mrs. Ware to come to the hospital, Mr. Ware. Her husband's taken a turn for the worse."

"Yes. Thank you." I hung up and turned to my mother. "Did you hear?"

She shook her head.

"It was Belmont. They said Dad's taken a turn for the worse and we should go to the hospital. They didn't say anything else."

Her face lost color but aside from that there was no sign.

"I'll get ready." She turned and started toward the bedroom.

"Mom?"

"Yes."

"We have to prepare ourselves. I doubt if they'd come right out and tell us on the phone. Do you know what I mean?"

"I understand Alan."

"Are you okay?"

She nodded.

Those neighbors who were out on their porches saw us back the car down the alley and into the street. This would mean only one thing to them. Without taking my eyes from the street I knew they were leaning forward, watching as we drove toward the corner.

I parked two blocks from the hospital, walked with my arm around her. We walked slowly, silently. There were no elderly people sitting in front of the apartment house now.

A narrow alley separated the apartment house from the nearest one-family residence. Thanks to venetian blinds that fit imperfectly a certain number of windows located on that otherwise darkened side of the apartment house which overlooked the alley were edged in light. These edges lit nothing, threw no light, did not combine in any obvious design. It struck me that this real-life construction might just as easily have been a cubist depiction of the crack of dawn.

"When we get upstairs why don't you wait in the lounge. I'll walk down to the nurse's station."

"All right."

I waited for a moment. She sat very rigidly, the only person in there. It was 11:30. Walking from the lounge to the nurse's station would involve passing my father's room.

The door was open, my father's bed empty, stripped of linen, a bare mattress, nothing else. Mr. Feeney was in the second bed, Mr. Rothstein in the third one.

"I'm Alan Ware. Mr. Ware's son."

"Oh," the nurse said, "stay right here. I'll get Dr. Sawyer." A moment later a doctor appeared. I spoke before he could say anything.

"My mother's in the lounge. Do you want me to get her?"

"No. We can speak down there."

My mother hadn't moved.

"I'm Dr. Sawyer. Mrs. Ware, your husband died at 9:50. I'd like to extend my condolences."

She nodded, acknowledging his words.

"We knew this was coming," I said.

If we were up to it, he said, there were some things he wanted to talk to us about. He suggested we take a few minutes to collect ourselves.

Then we answered questions. We didn't yet know when the funeral would be or which funeral home would be in charge. He recommended that an autopsy be performed but after some discussion we vetoed that idea.

I picked up the phone and dialed.

"Carol?"

"Yes."

"It's Alan."

"Oh." There was a long pause. "Hi."

"Dad died."

"Poor thing. When?"

"Tonight."

There was silence.

"Did he suffer much?"

"Yes." I waited. "The funeral's the day after tomorrow."

There was silence, then she said, "Alan, I can't come in."

"I just thought you'd want to know."

"Sure. I appreciate your calling. Should I say something to Rose?"

"She's in bed now. We had to make quite a few calls when we got back from the hospital. I just thought you'd want to know."

"Alan, I'm sorry."

The following morning I called Monadnock and told the people there just what the situation was. Together we decided that my visit, which had already been delayed, should begin in two weeks.

* * * *

At thirty-eight I remain a writer with only the slightest, most local of reputations.

My father's dying, I'd thought at one time, guaranteed a story. Consequently I accused myself: Parasite, you goddamn parasite. The accusation was nonsense, a misrepresentation; nevertheless, at Monadnock I discovered that before I could do anything with his death I had to overcome the fear of having been parasitical in my approach to it. Eventually that happened.

And there have been other changes too. I'm married now. I have a child.

Last year when Anne was two she'd walk by a mirror, see herself, and think she was seeing someone else. Perhaps that's a problem that runs in the family. Though I saw my father as reduced at times, though at other times I saw him as enlarged, the fact is in certain critical ways when I looked at my father I saw myself.

As for my mother, well, that's strange. Little has been resolved in the time that's passed since my father's death. With the neighborhood in flux, though the character of the neighborhood changes, she remains. I'm uneasy about this, of course, as is she, but when I ask her, Isn't it dangerous to still be here, she says she doesn't feel threatened, at least not yet.

Neighborhood stores that close don't reopen. If there's a fire in a building on the avenue, the building's boarded up, not repaired. Yet it's not all bleak.

A few weeks after my father's death my mother told me that she received a handwritten note from Silverman expressing sympathy. And she heard from Dr. Harris, a condolence card postmarked Albuquerque. Lou said she was working at a clinic on an Indian reservation.

Funded in large part by federal money, centers for people over sixty had opened in neighborhoods all over New York. The East Flatbush Adult Center was housed in the basement of a synagogue just four blocks from home. After an appropriate period of time my mother, urged by family and some neighbors, joined.

"This way you get dressed every day. It gets you out of the house." In talking to me about it she sounded slightly defensive at first. "There's a hot meal at noon, which is more than I'd make for myself, and if anyone can't afford the twenty-five cents you'd still get the meal, believe me."

"It sounds good."

But there were drawbacks.

The vast majority of people who go there are widows, she said. "And just to be with old people everyday, that isn't healthy. Still, for the time being it's as good as can be."

And that's where it stands except for the dimension that has been added. At the center she makes belts and bibs for our daughter, her granddaughter, and she hopes for more grandchildren.

Now that Anne is three there's a conversation that we have, in one form or another, a couple of times a day.

Daddy, she asks when I come home or when I step out of the bathroom, will you play with me?

Sure.

You be the teacher.

Okay. Who do you want to be?

Dulcy.

Good. Dulcy, this is first grade. We're going to do math today. How much is one plus one?

Sitting straight in her small chair she purses her lips and looks thoughtful.

I mouth the answer: two.

Two, Teacher.

Good, Dulcy. Now how much is two plus two?

Daddy, be my Daddy again. No, be a baby. I'll be the mommy.

Okay. Hello, Mommy. I'm a baby.

Baby, are you hungry?

Yes. Can I have something to eat, Mommy?

Sure. But nothing sweet.

Okay. Mommy, I want to tell you something. I have a secret.

She comes close and I ask in a whisper, Mommy can I have a Popsicle?

Baby, she looks shocked, you didn't eat lunch yet.

I didn't?

No. But that's okay. You can have a Popsicle.

Thank you, Mommy.

You want rootbeer?

I love rootbeer.

The rootbeer's all gone. You want orange?

This conversation will go on as long as I let it, and I enjoy it, I'm patient. I want her to have what I didn't have as well as all that I did have. In idle moments I wonder, What can I provide to make up for the bad example set by my father, the example I hope I've learned something from?

When it dawned on me that when looking at him I saw myself, the story of his death became mine, and if questions remain about my behavior I know that it's in the writing of my fiction that those questions will be addressed.

I now know any number of things that I should have known all along. I now know that some mistakes are not rectifiable. I now know that initiation, which is a big thing in my line of work, is ongoing, lifelong, not something that occurs and then it's over and done with.

Now I think of feeling unfulfilled and shake my head in wonder. Alan, I now say to myself, what in the hell is wrong with you? Life is not orgasmic. Why would you expect to feel fulfilled, or satisfied? Who's been feeding you that line? You might as well let it get you down that you don't feel complete, but that's not in the cards either. *Life* is complete, and we have death to thank for that. In lieu of completion we accumulate a history; that's my sense of things, anyway. The lines that show on my face aren't a mask; they aren't a cover-up. I know that. Forces work on me. I change. I find that I am unexpectedly capacious.

Of course there are regrets. I regret that I'll never be one of those two-fisted writers I've so much admired. But I'm pleased that I've been able to pursue my ambition. And I'm satisfied with Level, with the way I earn my living, with my family. I'm satisfied that, after struggling, after floundering, I'm close to finishing the fiction that my father plays a role in. I don't have hopes for it so much as attitudes about it, which range from, Here's fiction the likes of which you haven't seen, to, My God, it's thin gruel. There are certain things I know beyond doubt. Of the sentences that work, most were earned, few inspired. Some creak. They were all influenced by the weather.

This fiction—this story I was guaranteed—became a burden I'm about to lay down, an obligation I'm about to fulfill. Rather than a matter of fate or hope it will be a matter of record.

And finally, for the record, I'd simply make this point: relative to the lives lived by other people, mine, up to now, has been a fairly good one.

The Family

Billy Butler, the lanky maintenance man sent by the Island to Savannah Airport to pick me up, supplemented what little information I had. No more than thirty or thirty-five people, including employees, ever stayed on the Island at any one time. The Island's only phone was in the compound, which was that area of Wither where the employees—the household staff and maintenance crew—lived. The employees also had homes on the mainland.

Billy Butler was the genuine article, an older version of the boys from Valdosta and Gadsden whom I'd been in the service with: shitkicking music and corn liquor, hunting and fishing and an uncompromised drawl. . . . At age fifty he appeared proper in faded denim plus boots run down at the heel yet with a swirl of fancy stitchwork where they ran up his leg.

We drove in an unmarked station wagon to the very outskirts of town, then turned onto a bumpy private road at the end of which was a dock; tied up at the dock was a launch. Billy, after seeing to the car, climbed aboard. I passed him my typewriter and suitcase and climbed aboard too. We cast off.

I took off my corduroy jacket, rolled up my sleeves, and, standing in the stern, felt expansive, felt a rather unfamiliar sense of contentment. Out in the channel I waved at occasional nearby craft. Billy was steady at the wheel. The water was calm, rippling, a shade of blue only slightly too dark to be transparent. At my back the mainland was receding.

After perhaps twenty silent minutes I made my way forward.

"Is that it?"

He nodded. "That's her. Won't be long now."

When we entered the shallows the color of the water had changed; here it was a straightforward muddy brown. The skimpy sand beach didn't do much for me either; nevertheless, even in the vicinity of the dock, elegant palm trees promised the exotic.

"Who's that?" I asked, referring to the man standing on the dock waving.

"The Director," he said.

I was waving back.

Dave Spinario shook my hand just moments after I stepped ashore.

"Welcome to Wither."

"Thanks. It's great to be here. This is fantastic."

I wanted to pause and survey the scene, but this graying, ruggedly handsome man in his late fifties, whose first name was the same as my father's, had already grabbed my suitcase, had turned his back to me, and was marching toward the VW microbus. As I hurried to catch up to him, he put me in mind, physically, of Caesar Romero.

It was a balmy, windless day. I bounced up and down on the front seat as we began the brief trip to the lodge.

"Did you have a good flight?"

"Fine."

He took a sharp right and suddenly we were driving parallel with the shoreline and perhaps seventy-five yards from it. To my untutored eye the area in between was marsh: high grass, water, and water birds. The scene was so steady and undramatic that had I come upon it gradually I might not have given it a second glance. Yet it was extraordinary. Like marshes on calendars it seemed an idealization; however, unlike those marshes the highlight here was not serenity. Its clarity was compelling, evidently independent of stillness, since in the midst of movement the clarity remained. When a gull rose from the grass and flew off, the line of flight, like a vapor trail, remained visible to me. A sense of things being tangible or graspable here swept over me. How paradoxical that now, although I felt acutely alone, the idea of establishing a relationship didn't appeal, not at all, no way. Tranquility appealed, tranquility and order.

"I like to let people take the Island in at their own pace. Sometimes it takes some getting used to."

Turning to respond, I was jarred by a new and incredible world some ten or twelve feet off the left side of the road. I saw clumps of squat palmetto: to me this screamed jungle.

Tranquility and order: it was as if I were being willfully perverse; *tranquility and order* with a marriage on the rocks, with matters I once thought of as resolved proving unresolvable.

Hard-packed dirt roads with oyster shell used as a kind of binding crisscrossed the Island's 30,000 acres, Dave said, adding, "That's just about the size of Bermuda."

"Bermuda, God."

It was staggering. It was as if bristling pineapple leaves had gone mad with growth. The trunks of these dwarf trees appeared surrealistically sheathed in giant, spikey palms, while other palms were interwoven with masses of tropical vine: one couldn't have been prepared for this. No lushness, no wildflowers, only a tangle of bush and vine ranging in color from light gray to darkest brown plus of course palm green.

Although vegetation didn't form a solid wall on this side of the road it was all shadow here, and hovering depths. Perhaps some seepage existed because in places the earth was an oozing, almost a bubbling black.

Attracted and repelled, I stared. This was jungle: the front line. Though it was probably pock-marked with interior spaces I felt that if you attempted to enter it, more than likely it would fall back upon itself into near impenetrability.

Dave was slowing the bus, pointing at a line of freshly turned earth just off the shoulder.

"You know what that is?" he asked.

To me it looked as if a person with a shovel had been at work.

"Wild pigs have been rooting here. We must have just missed them."

I tried to communicate nonchalance. "Oh really? Wild pigs?"

What the hell was I doing here? This wasn't my milieu.

I was even uncertain of the sincerity of my dockside enthusiasm, suspecting it had been partially manufactured, obligatory, nothing more than a matter of good manners.

"That's home," he said, "up ahead."

Acknowledging the role of application and qualification, still I wondered how—how, in other words, in the grand scheme of things—had I come to be sitting here in a room that was the size of any ballroom or hotel lobby—my bags already upstairs—listening as Dave presented what was clearly the ritual precautionary talk: when I'm out walking if I see a rotting log lying across a path turn back, report it, the staff will remove it, don't try to climb over it, that's just asking for trouble. What kind? Snakes: copperhead, cottonmouth. . . . Always, *always* stick to the path, don't wander into the palmetto because getting lost would be dangerous. And then after that there was this: never place a bull in a situation where he feels cornered. When I realized what he'd just said I chose not to pursue it. Loggerhead turtles, alligators, donkeys: a fair number of animals live on the Island, it's more their Island than ours, that's the philosophy here, so give them plenty of elbow room. And finally: shortly before dinner guests generally gather downstairs for a drink. No one's obligated to make an appearance, all that we insist on is that you show up for your meals on time. Any questions? Good. Then why don't you get yourself settled, you probably want to wash up. He showed me to my second-floor room, a well-appointed studio bedroom with French doors that opened onto a balcony where I stood thinking, So this is how the moneyed class lives. I immediately was unhappy with myself for thinking that. It was a hostile thought, the thought of an ingrate. I stepped back. You have misgivings, I told myself, you feel menaced, relax. There's no need to unpack right this minute, go out.

I got sidetracked en route. I poked around on the first floor and managed to locate the sun-room, the library, the laundry and shell rooms, plus, next to the kitchen, the room with the loom, the weaver's studio. Outside, however, it was different. I was cautious and tentative. The lodge, a rectangular two-story structure that was vaguely Spanish in appearance with its stucco exterior and tiled roof, I studied while standing on an expanse of casually tended front lawn, the kind on which you'd want to spread a blanket before sitting. Together with a fringe of marsh this was all that lay between the lodge and the water.

Right now with the tide rising the marsh was partially underwater. I turned back, not ready to venture beyond the immediate grounds.

Back in my room, sitting on the side of the bed taking off my shoes, I discovered stickers or burrs the size of jelly beans stuck to the bottom few inches of my pants. I folded several pieces of toilet paper for protection and after gingerly removing the burrs flushed them down the toilet. A private bathroom: not bad. I ran a bath and when I finished drying, walked back into the room naked with the idea of unpacking. I stepped toward the suitcase: a sudden sting, pain, it was sharp, a bite. I'd been bitten, I realized, on the sole of my foot; it burned. Next I discovered myself leaning on the dresser attempting to balance on one leg so that I might raise my foot. Though I was prepared for a dot or smear of blood on my sole, actually I was frightening myself, picturing all manner of things: that I'd been stung, for instance, by some kind of tropical bug, which probably wasn't completely impossible here. It was reasonable and even prudent to be frightened but on another level the more frightened I was the better it would be for me because that way the relief would be sweeter because after all I really couldn't have been bitten by a deadly bug or spider, that was outlandish, not me, I was from Brooklyn a writer-professor-visitor hopping naked on my good foot to a wicker chair to lift my foot bending to see I saw it was still on me almost shouting panicked a kind of primal terror sweeping through me kicking my foot out wildly to shake it off some sort of vicious leachlike organism had clamped itself onto me, sunk its teeth into me, sucking, poisoning me, God. . . .

During those blind explosive moments when I tried to kick not only a bug but even my leg free of my body I'd somehow been lucky enough to avoid hurting my knee. When rationality returned I raised my foot and forced myself to look. There was no insect. As it turned out I'd carried burrs into the room on the soles of my shoes; a few had rubbed off on the rug and it was on one of those that I'd stepped.

Exhausted: God was I exhausted.

I lay down, slept.

A couple of hours later, while dressing, I resolved I'd do better. After all, being an unknown quantity here was actually an opportunity, something to be seized upon, tantamount to starting out with a clean slate; therefore, why not assume a sociable demeanor, why not demonstrate poise? Of course, don't come on *too* strong. At 5:30 I left my room, ready to meet for the first time and mingle with the other guests.

I stopped on the second-floor landing, casually stood at the railing in view of whoever might look up in order that I might take in all that was below. It was by means of no discernible formula that this room, whose dimensions I couldn't make a stab at, implied a style of living that, in its elegance, was far removed from the rustic outdoorsy style in which the room itself was done, so that despite the exposed beams that crossed the ceiling, despite the stuffed animal heads mounted on its walls, it might hold ladies in long dresses, which two of the women *were* wearing, and men in suits made by the finest tailors, which none of these men likely was wearing, without some third party ever feeling those people had gathered together in celebration of a particular occasion.

I stopped again at the foot of the stairs, this time appearing to think about a rather elaborately designed circular wall hanging directly in front of me.

In fact the pattern was set. It was to be by starts and stops that I'd navigate this room. My subsequent show of interest in the framed and fading legal documents pertaining to the Island, the paintings, the glass-eyed fish and family photos, all of which were mounted and hanging on walls, was strategic, a way to present myself as someone fully at ease.

An older man sidled up to me. "It's a gallery of assorted treasures." He'd detached himself only at the very last moment from the group of people I'd been moving inevitably toward.

"Amazing. I'm Alan Ware."

"Frank Hodgkiss. Glad to meet you."

Since Dave wasn't present, Frank handled the introductions. There were eight or nine people down here.

"Michael Flynn, Roberta DeMarco, Alan Ware."

"Hi."

Before he steered me away from Olympia Paige, a grandmotherly woman from Providence, Rhode Island, I learned that after years of writing children's books she was now attempting a novel. Frank was on his third visit since retiring as chairman of the art department at a small Ohio college.

Well-worn maroon velour drapes emphasized the royal-hunting-lodge aspect of the place; nevertheless, the several plain and comfortable couches seemed to fit, as did the leather armchairs of the sort one imagined elderly Englishmen with nostalgia for the Empire falling asleep in.

"And that's Phil Stallings," Frank said. The man who'd just placed a log in the fireplace half turned and nodded; a moment later he added kindling and soon there was a blaze.

Drinking someone's Rebel Yell, I chatted easily. Stallings worked in neon and plexiglass. I moved to a window seat, pleased.

Then Dave came down and very shortly afterward we were on our way to the dining room. Dave's appearance, considering what he was up against—a sky blue shirt with a ruffled front and string tie, plus a turquoise belt buckle—was impressive, like that of the successful rancher who on his visits to New York makes sure to take in the season's hit shows.

"Have you met everyone?" he asked.

"Yes."

Because of my newcomer status I sat next to him during the meal.

Like a long conference table but with beveled edges and stout, elaborately carved legs, this dining room table with chairs more ornate than any you'd ever sit on in your own home seemed appropriate here, as did the tiled fireplace, as did the low-hanging chandelier, as did the little silver bell beside Dave's plate which he'd tinkle whenever he wanted the attention of Verna Jones or Lucille Grayson or Mandy Childs, the kitchen staff. Often as not Billy and Verna's lame brother, Hoyt, who every morning carried in an armload of firewood, would be hanging around in the kitchen at this time, drinking coffee and smoking Camels, content just to stay out of harm's way, there ultimately to drive the women back to the compound when everything was done.

We took coffee in the main room, a sensible practice since it allowed the staff to finish up a bit earlier than they otherwise might and it was in here that the trouble, with roots that could be traced to the dining room, occurred.

I was no judge; nevertheless, in the way one never got over suspecting middle-level Chinese bigwigs of lining their drab proletarian outfits with lavishly brocaded material, I suspected my behavior had been more complicated than it may have appeared.

Since I *was* no judge, and therefore not immune to the consequences of mistakes in judgment, I was vulnerable. It was now sometime after eleven, maybe near midnight. I was lying in bed in my darkened room uncovering motives and in this roundabout fashion exploring the extent of my vulnerability.

During dinner conversation had been carried on with the person next to or across from you, in my case with Wendy Burke, whose face was familiar not only because I'd seen it in 1930s Depression photos but more recently and repeatedly in the waiting room of Greyhound bus stations, the drab young wife of the soldier or sailor who's gone for a couple of hot dogs; she's contending with a crying baby, trying to get a pacifier into the baby's mouth; somehow the stringy blond hair is appropriate to the long narrow face with thin lips, boney jaw, and flat blue eyes. Against all odds Wendy doesn't come from Kentucky, however, but from California, a rich man's daughter.

Here she can make her own vegetable dyes, she told me; that's what makes Wither so marvelous for a weaver.

Dave was preoccupied during the first part of the meal; he remained so until perhaps the midpoint when he told us he'd be spending a couple of days at a time in Savannah and Atlanta these next few months because, he explained, politics was rearing its head: developers wanted the Island and the county, in collusion with them, had, for instance, rezoned the Island upward making taxes ridiculously high. When he was through we asked questions. Not Frank. He assured Dave that in the final analysis the powers that be would recognize the Island's value to the area, even to the region.

Frank began warming to the task. "It's been my experience," he said, "that after everything's said and done public officials generally have the good of the people at heart."

I simply hadn't been able to let that go by.

In bed I berated myself: asshole. It was as if he'd suckered me into making a fool of myself.

No. Although I realized it only now, what he'd really done was hand me just the excuse I'd been looking for.

First I indicated differences existed between us by saying in a skeptical voice, "I don't know, Frank."

Then I launched into what I announced would be a true story, and I really laid it on. Since almost everyone wanted coffee, almost everyone was subjected to it: how my mother and I, with my father bleeding and cancer-ridden, had been treated with callous disregard that morning we'd arrived at the doctor's office ready to okay a second operation. Parallels, I assumed, would surely be drawn between that incident and the matter at hand: public officials and, from my perspective, *their* contempt for the public.

As I lay in bed, however, baser motives emerged. Undoubtedly I'd seen that under the guise of answering Frank I'd be able to unburden myself of the incident, and the exhibitionist in me had a field day doing it. Also, ever the opportunist, I sensed there existed in that incident the potential for establishing my quote real-world bona fides, something certain of us who nest in the ivory tower sometimes feel a need to do: I come from a life, I thought the incident would imply, where day-to-day living could at any time include poor treatment, struggle.

I squirmed, remembering it all, especially the awkward embarrassed silence during and right after the outburst.

When it was over Dave was the first to say something. "Well," he said, "I think I'll call it a night."

No chance for misinterpretation there.

In hopes of putting this out of my mind I decided to get out of bed. Maybe read. I turned on the bedside light then resisted the urge to snap it right off. Instead I watched six or eight or ten two-inch-long black palmetto roaches rush along the floor feeling for a crack of darkness to disappear into.

As predictable as Lutheran ministers going off on summertime junkets to the Holy Land, breakfast the next morning went off without reference to the events of the night before. With that end in mind guests at the breakfast table had applied a familiar formula: they made me, in effect, invisible. Being in a body the mass of which had not evaporated, I reacted by taking seconds of everything: eggs, sausage, grits, coffee.

"Great meal," I said as I made ready to push away from the table.

"Now I guess it's time to get to it."

And with that I returned to my room.

An hour or an hour and a half later, frustrated, I let myself out of the room thinking, I'll pace the hallway. Near the end of the hall a door stood open. I looked and then on impulse moved into the doorway.

"What can I do for you?" Dave asked.

"Nothing really."

"You want a cup of coffee?"

"Sure."

After sitting down, feeling the need to say something, I said, "Has it been your experience that some people—are there some people who never adjust to this place?"

"A few. It isn't for everyone. How's everything going?"

I nodded. "Okay."

His short-sleeve shirt was archetypal: busy with buttons and snappy creases, tan, with shoulder straps bars or stars could be pinned on. For all of that he wasn't headquartered in Nairobi or on safari, he was sitting behind a cluttered desk in a cramped cubbyhole of an office doing paperwork.

"Thanks," I said, taking the coffee he handed me; then I concentrated on stirring the coffee and blowing on it.

"If you need anything, don't be afraid to ask."

"Dave"—Billy Butler knocked on the door even as he was barging in—"that goll-danged fool in the Garage—." Then he saw me. The Garage had been converted to a painter's studio.

"What happened?" Dave asked.

Billy's reluctance was obvious.

"Look," I put my nearly full coffee cup down, "I was just on my way to check this place out so I'll see both of you later."

"Which way you heading?" Dave asked.

"No idea."

"Okay, but keep your eyes open. Be alert."

In a hurry I returned to my room, changed into boots, then rubbed mosquito repellant on my arms and neck. Outside I chose the first path I came to, one that started near the shoreline, and plunged inland.

Behind the gum and oak that stood like sentinels on either side of this path the vegetation seemed rather sparse, the density no greater than that on a checkerboard with half the board empty. Since the path ran parallel to the immediate grounds, I managed to maintain direct eye contact with various of the out-buildings. Then the path began twisting. As it narrowed I began to feel the jungle closing in, squeezing. Trees that had lined the path now arched overhead, forming a canopy, blocking out light. Stopping, looking around, intent, it seemed, on inducing anxiety, I finally focused on a live oak from whose middle branches a conical-shaped vine was hanging, but unattractively, patternlessly, a self-entangled mess, like a child's abandoned scribbling.

Next time I'll pack sandwiches and go on a real walk, a hike, I thought, not so much making plans for the future as laying the groundwork for a quick return to the lodge. For the time being, though, I continued and within a matter of minutes came to a roadside pond. It was filled with brackish water. This lifted my spirits. To have something to do I tossed a rock in and it sank, leaving a dark hole in the green slime. I tossed a handful of pebbles high in the air, and when they showered down there wasn't a drop of musical effect to the splashing. I whipped around but then didn't know which way to look or even what it was I'd heard. Oh boy.

Now I moved along the light-dappled oyster-shell path as I might walk through a glass-littered Brooklyn alley: much of the time anxiously looking back over my shoulder and it was after negotiating a slight jog in the path in this manner, then turning to look straight ahead, that I got the shock of my life: the path was thick with deer, the large one that was closest to me no further from me than a person might be from the TV set in his living room. I was frozen to the spot, in a state of temporary paralysis. The question of what *I* ought to do never even presented itself. My first clear thought was, Face facts, you're not at the zoo, this is precisely what it appears to be but wouldn't it have been normal for the eight or nine deer blocking my path to bolt. The large one looked at me with dark, liquid eyes, the others never even looked; without interruption they moseyed along, mouths to the ground, nibbling until at long last the large one slowly moved from my path and one by one at a leisurely pace the others followed into the jungle, loping, gathering themselves into a pack. I felt excitement increasing in direct proportion to the increase in the distance between us. Now, like a baserunner caught in a rundown, I was running back and forth on the path in search of any spot that offered an unobstructed view of the jungle's depths, wanting to keep them in sight for as long as possible.

Nevertheless, they were quickly gone from sight, but the rush of feeling that had come over me persisted. It wasn't merely a matter of relief either. Without even thinking about it I understood that now I could turn back; but now I didn't want to. Barely able to contain my elation, for ten minutes or more I walked along the path observing next to nothing.

Then partway across a rickety bridge that spanned a slowly moving stream I stopped and turned to the rail; here I fell prey to the observation deck syndrome: intent as an Audubon warden, an instant Leatherstocking, I sought out detail, my eyes returning again and again to an area on the surface of the water that appeared particularly dark, made dark not by an oil slick or anything of that sort; rather, it was as if something were submerged immediately below the surface. There were two tree stumps and some high grass in the shallow water near this spot, which in its outline conformed to the posture a person would assume when doing the dead man's float. Though it might be an underwater rock formation or a log lodged among rocks, there was a more likely explanation: alligator.

This was an alligator lair. After once again scanning the surface of the water I trained my eyes on all likely locations near the shoreline. In the process of satisfying myself that no alligators were sunning on the bank I spotted something half buried in the mud.

I felt a compulsion to investigate. A proprietary interest had been aroused. On the basis of a knowledge I'd never acquired, with a confidence I simply accepted, I crossed the bridge, scouted around, and found a few feet from the path a torn-up plank which I hoisted onto my shoulder and carried back across the bridge. Then I made my way down the sloping bank until the footing became uncertain, at which point I dropped the plank in front of myself. I stepped on it; it didn't sink under my weight. Proceeding cautiously I made my way to the end of the plank, knelt, then like a pianist about to begin, extended my arms and a moment later lowered them. The sun was hot on the back of my neck. The alligator was twenty feet from me. My fingers made contact with the moist, grainy muck, which yielded under pressure, my fingers sinking to the first joints, the second. There was the urge to plunge down to my wrist, and that wasn't complete craziness either; I could then tunnel under the object and scoop it up. Instead I withdrew my right hand, raised and positioned it, then closed my eyes, held my breath, and softly, very softly, brought it down on top of the half-buried object just as I was bringing my left hand up underneath it. I had it, was raising it, holding it as far from my body as humanly possible, euphoric and repulsed at the same time. My God, I had a skull in my hands, a skull, the eye sockets, the lower jaw, everything.

"Look," I yelled, instantly subverting my wish to be matter-of-fact. "Hey, Dave."

He was alone on the patio. "Say, where'd you get that?" He put aside the net he'd been using to clean the outdoor aquarium.

I motioned with my head. "Back there. What do you make of this?"

"It's a pig's skull, you can tell from the elongated jaw, see. Come on."

He held the screen door open, then led me to the shell room where he took the skull from me.

"Are they rare or plentiful or what?"

"Depends on what you mean by plentiful. I wouldn't say our guests normally go around tripping over them. You've got yourself an unusual souvenir."

"No way. It's yours." He looked at me. "I'm giving it to you. You keep extra typewriters on hand for writers, right? Painters might want to use this in a still life."

"Well, we'll talk about it."

"There's nothing to talk about," I said.

He was rinsing the skull in one of the two basins in this double sink. I scrubbed my hands as if for surgery.

"You know, Alan," he was now taking a wet cloth to it "it's not a good idea to leave the path."

I wasn't sure if that was spoken in reprimand or not. Don't be paranoid, I thought, he's right.

"I guess I got excited."

"There," he said. "Now that's damn near human looking, isn't it."

"I have a feeling even a human skull wouldn't strike me as very human. This is an area I don't have much experience in, but sure there's a resemblance. I see what you're saying."

"Something like this makes you think," he said.

"Really? About what?"

"For one thing, that it would be a crime if we ever lose this Island."

After last night I didn't want to get started on that again.

That afternoon, in the flush of redemption, I approached my work eagerly. I worked well and soon fell into a satisfactory daily rhythm: writing a few hours in the morning, a few hours after lunch, and occasionally a bit more at night. My primary reason for being here was, after all, to accomplish something, to move ahead on my book. If during the preceding months I'd accommodated an inability to concentrate by writing on the run, by taking notes and jotting phrases, I couldn't afford such accommodation again. Here on Wither I simply had to write.

With Wither restricted to people engaged in one way or another in the arts, what we did not have here was an *omnium gatherum;* still, variety existed; however, an average stay at Wither probably ran no more than two weeks. So just as there are people at a party whom you mean to talk to, the lawyer representing Mercy Hospital in its malpractice suits, for instance, but circumstance prevents it—he leaves early or you get involved with someone in the kitchen—so it was on the Island.

Among the guests who came and went during my stay were those who diverted their eyes and stared into corners. Equally, there were women who as a political act hadn't shaved their legs for an inordinate period of time. Floyd Danielson, the writer, read one of his stories aloud late one chilly November night and showed how, by invoking the magic of his art, a stunning and dramatic real-life incident could be transformed, made into something boring and inane. Martin Mandel was an irascible forty-year-old bachelor who on occasion, if he wanted to impress or get laid, was capable of demonstrating charm and wit. While I could never figure out what he did, it did have a name: mixed media. Along with a university-imprinted poet there was a sculptor with a smile like a rubber band stretched to its limit who saw one of the women with hairy legs, a novelist, sunbathing on the patio and then spoke to me like a comrade: My dick's so hard I got a headache, he said, hairy legs turn me on, how about you?

Although I saw those people with a satiric eye, I counted myself among them. As for the satiric eye, seen socioeconomically it merely reflected a lower-middle-class attitude I never could quite shake and perhaps hinted of a feeling I harbored toward myself, or why at times I grunted and grimaced in an attempt to inflate certain muscles: why else but to assure myself regarding choices long since made.

Become secure early in my stay by the reestablishment of a workmanlike routine, a routine that held for the remainder of my stay, no longer pressured by my environment, I remained, nevertheless, less than amiable; I was brusque. Guests made every effort to tolerate each other's particular requirements and people gave me room, more room in fact than I necessarily wanted.

At a point when I'd seen—but hadn't yet mustered the courage to get up on—the exercise bicycle located on the cement apron at the side of the lodge, seeing people on the patio eating lunch, with motives innocent of ill intent, with a motive as benign as wishing for some human contact, I took my tray of sandwich, fruit, and coffee from the kitchen and went out.

Thelma McVey, who'd arrived on the Island after I had, patted the chair next to hers. "Sit down."

"Take a load off your feet," said Henry Tamarik.

"Hi. Thanks."

"You think he tears around the Island in the pickup," Thelma said, "watch out when he's driving the jeep." Thelma had been here before.

"You talking about Dave?" I asked.

"Who else?" Tom said, and they laughed.

There was a sudden impulse, which I checked, to bad-mouth Dave. He was known for his driving. This was something I'd been hearing about ever since my arrival. Somehow I was sure that back on the mainland Mrs. McVey was not so tolerant of reckless drivers.

"He didn't drive all that crazily when he picked me up at the dock," I said.

"That's business," Tom said. "Watch out when he's driving for pleasure."

How, I wondered, can you develop antipathy for someone you've been given no reason to feel antipathetic toward, unless of course you can't.

After a few more minutes of their conversation I realized I had my nose out of joint. I said things to annoy the people at the table. I told them I found donkeys braying at night a real pain in the ass. I said that in my opinion the reason there were no flowers around was because the fucking animals ate the flowers. "But that's neither here nor there," I said, standing, excusing myself, stretching and walking toward the side of the lodge to get away, to think clearly.

There it was.

I climbed on the exercise bicycle as naturally as the child whose mother puts ten cents or a quarter in the slot climbs on the mechanical horse in front of K-Mart.

Immediately I recognized this as my cup of tea, a solitary endeavor that left me free to think or blank out, either one.

There had been something ambiguous, something enigmatic, something private and ironic, something exclusive even of me in Dave's intercourse with me so far, and by God, I thought as I pedaled, it really must have gotten under my skin.

Once a week a launch took guests into town for the day. This schedule was adhered to with a single exception: in mid-November we had two days of hurricane-like weather and no boats ran. Whenever I went into Savannah I called Brooklyn, and during more than one of those calls my habit of riding the exercise bicycle gave us a good laugh. The message from my mother was always the same: she was feeling fine. I would assure her that the same held true for me. Not absolutely so.

One brilliantly clear and crisp afternoon shortly after Dave, who lived in the room next to mine, returned from the mainland with the Island's mail, I learned of, I received official notification of, my divorce. It *was* true that, two exceptions granted, I pretty effectively put aside that news, at least in terms of an immediate reaction. The public expression or venting of emotion came late that night. After hours of struggle I unlocked the door to my room, then opened my bathroom door, bent over the toilet bowl, and roared into it, pretending to vomit. As if the nausea were coming in wave after wave I roared and flushed and roared and flushed some more. The next day, claiming illness, I skipped breakfast, and that night in the dining room the first thing I said was, "Anyone else get this bug that's going around? It must be the twenty-four-hour flu."

In addition, I conceded another day or so's writing time to the news, but of course a sore throat could cost me that, or certainly the televising of the state high school basketball tournament, an annual daytime-nighttime Friday-Saturday affair. Otherwise, with my time here growing short, I went on as before.

And yet not quite as before.

Cane Patch Beach, which was splendid and wild, was well on the other side of the Island, eight miles away perhaps, a good forty-minute drive. We could go there only when Dave drove, and when we went we would spend the best part of the day. He scheduled a trip every ten days or so. I took advantage of the first few opportunities, then, begrudging the time, skipped the next couple. News of the divorce made me want to return. Weather intervened. Heavy rains had the roads impassable; after that a spell of cold and especially windy weather led to cancellations.

I hadn't screamed into the toilet bowl because the news was now final but because my sense of the situation lay in quite the opposite direction. It didn't seem final, it wasn't concluded, not to me, yet there it was in black and white staring me in the face. I couldn't reconcile myself. Were my feelings misleading me and if that was the case then where did I stand, because what could I trust when it came to my writing if not my feelings: this could mean trouble ahead. Fortunately, in matters of such magnitude, I was resourceful.

As gold was free from liability to rust, so I was not golden, I knew that. After a certain stage in life I believed that innocence was something for which a person ought to be held culpable. There were bare-chested molders of character who cried, Show me a good loser and I'll show you a loser. Show me a winner, I would say in answer to that. For all that tough thinking of mine, it wasn't in order to swim that I wanted to return to the beach—the water would be too cold—but for the cheap satisfaction of it: after all, I too went to Hollywood movies. I wanted to treat myself to the picture I would make tramping by the water's edge, solitary, melancholic, the whole enchilada. There would be, I thought, a kind of sustenance in that.

Accordingly, when beach day came I was one of the seven people who piled into the bus. Down Hellhole Road we drove, over to Mule Run, past Suckhead Spit and Buckhead Marsh, finally parking in a clearing that overlooked the beach. It was in the seventies with the sun ducking in and out.

I took off my shoes and prepared for the occasional splash of incoming waves on my ankles by rolling my pants to the calf. It was traditional for guests to strike out on their own at the beach, or in pairs. When I was nearly an hour into my walk I was quite sure no one was ahead of me and that was how I wanted it. Aside from the fact that with the tide out it was unpleasantly slimy underfoot, the day was going very well. When I'd stamp my foot on the hard-packed sand, sandcrabs, like miniature grasshoppers, jumped theatrically. Scrawny cows strayed from the palmetto that fringed the beach, but they didn't stray very far. I hadn't forgotten my purpose in coming, nor did I feel it necessary to push. Now dead as a doornail, the size of homeplate, a horseshoe crab had washed ashore; I stood over it but came to no conclusions. Then in the distance I saw a tree located, in relation to the water, where a lifeguard's stand might be had this been a public beach. Nothing near it. Though still standing it was in fact the remains of a tree, the raw material of exotic giftstore driftwood. While that might have been a correct assessment of its future, right now as I saw it—it was stark and skeletal, the broken trunk and bleached white limbs, as if sculpted, twisting from the sand; it was in terrible angularity, the limbs flung; it was the posture of pain, the posture of an agony. Closer, closer, staring without choice, the boaters now shut from my view, the gulls, the dunes, the sea oats gone, my approach quickening, on the very verge of rushing as one rushes with mounting dread to the scene of a certain kind of accident, and actually it wasn't until I'd drawn to within twenty or twenty-five feet of this tree that it lost its human design and its power over me.

Though my heart was still pounding I passed by it as if it were a utility pole, but after I'd gone another few steps I doubled back. I made myself run my hand over its trunk and limbs as if there might be a message in Braille here, but there was no message for me; the tree made no impression; I was entirely settled again; it was as if nothing had happened.

I was about to continue my walk when I jumped back behind this tree, as if in hiding.

Out in waist-high water there was Dave coming in, not splashing, not shaking, proceeding in, the hair that covered the surface of his body wetted down—creating, from this distance, the impression of scaliness. There was bulk; there was solidity; there was grace. He was imposing, powerful, an unhurried figure of a man coming out of the water naked, or nearly so, wearing only the briefest of bathing suits as if he belonged on the Riviera or in an Italian movie. I stared from my spot, turned, then started to run quickly in the opposite direction.

Like any day at the beach, at Brighton or Jones Beach, for instance, if one leaves without first showering, having been worked on by sun and salt air, if one is sweaty with, as in my case, a powdery film of sand not only on the clothes but also on the skin, then, as I found after making a place for myself in a dune-like spot where water lapped onto the beach, regardless of what else may have transpired—you may have seen the rescue squad revive a middle-aged bather or played frisbee with a beautiful woman whom you'd never before seen or picked up a splinter on the way to the concession stand—no matter what, on the drive home if you're not the driver you're going to contend with grogginess. Grogginess hit me when I stopped moving, when I sat in my dune-like spot; I couldn't blink it away or stretch it away. I ate my sandwich and cookies but couldn't eat it away, so I quit, lay down, slept.

Woke up choking, my throat clogged, locked, no air, no air, then somehow I was sucking it in, frantically, noisily, a harrowing music, the noise of a child repeatedly inhaling on his first harmonica. My heart pounding again, taking a long time to slow down. I wanted to rest, to completely catch my breath, but still I stood up, it seemed safer. Christ, what a fucking day.

Nor was it over.

On the ride home Inez Porter was asking questions. I tried to tune out. In Level during the winter when the indoor air was dry, I remembered sometimes waking up choking at night gasping for air.

"Will you be going into Savannah Thursday?" she asked me.

Silently I shook my head.

"You're not?"

"No."

"I am. I love the spirit those people have."

"Inez, Savannah sucks and everyone knows it. You spend a day there and they yessir you to death. I hate that shit. Cabdrivers hustle you there just like they do everywhere else, don't they? You understand what I'm saying?"

"Are you serious?"

"Am I serious? You've got it the wrong way. Are *you* serious?"

"Alan, *Alan*," Dave called from the driver's seat.

"Yes Dave. Yes Dave."

"That skull of yours. I've been meaning to talk to you about it. It's still on the table in the shell room. What are you going to do with it?"

"I'm done with it. I told you, Dave, that's your skull," I said, pleased that though there was no particular meaning to what I'd just said, other than the obvious, it had a certain cryptic ring.

A half hour later we were back at the lodge, and the next day Dave left on another one of his trips.

I had but a week remaining.

Billy Butler would often be on the cement apron servicing one of the Island's vehicles when I'd arrive for my ride. For weeks now he'd been making friendly, ironic comments about the bike.

"Shoot, that dang thing's as useless as teats on a boar hog," Billy might say as he lifted the hood of the jeep.

Generally we could make out the sound but not the words of conversation coming from the patio, and somehow this had fostered a certain sense of camaraderie.

He was now sliding out from under the pickup.

"I'm going to miss this baby," I said. I'd just finished an hour on the bike. "You ought to give it a whirl, Billy." He looked directly at me.

"I'd rather build myself a wooden bill and pick shit with the chickens then set out knowing beforehand that even if I get where I'm going I won't be getting anywhere."

"Didn't you ever run in place?"

"Anytime I did it wasn't because I wanted to. Down here we don't roller skate on dirt roads neither."

"I think you know more than you're letting on, Billy, a lot more."

"Tell you what, I sure do miss that Eighth Avenue poon. Lord-a-mercy, that set a man right. I remember one old gal named Gladys. I believe she had an iron pussy."

He'd spent some time in New York on the way home from Korea. "Oh, *that* Gladys," I said. "Hell, she's still around."

I'd overdone it by biking for an hour. This was no surprise since for a while now I'd been wired.

"Man," I said to Billy, "I better walk this ride off. See you later."

Of late my only incentive for entering the jungle, which I'd come to look upon as an outdoor track, was to jog a bit, or if I'd biked to excess, to walk until overheated thigh and calf muscles cooled down. Having thus domesticated the jungle, fifteen or twenty minutes into my walk I wasn't on the alert for jungle sounds, for that sound in the distance that kept growing louder, getting closer until it was almost on me, a roaring, I stopped, turned, disoriented, moved without thinking from the path to the shoulder and no wonder, it was Dave in the jeep rounding a corner he had no right taking at such speed, straightening it out hunched over the wheel, riding the shoulder, bearing down, still on the shoulder—.

I jumped clear. I really hadn't been in danger. I'd had time. I'd exaggerated the whole thing by diving and now by remaining face down in the palmetto like a football player taking an extra moment on the turf after a hard tackle.

"Hey, you all right?"

The sponginess of this soil surprised me. I sat up. The heels of my palms were stained with dirt, and scraped. I brushed my shirt off.

"Yeah," I called back, "I think so."

He remained in the jeep looking back at me from the front seat as if I were a hitchhiker who was supposed to run to the car, say thanks, and jump right in. Why should I let him off the hook that easily. Let him sweat a little. Maybe I was hurt.

Then a wave. He was waving. A wave and a beep. He was gunning it. I was up on my feet. That fucking prick: he was gone and suddenly I was running away from the path, plunging, headlong, my legs rubber, weak, gasping, this was the way to lose myself, outrun the fear with roots like tripwire that I had to jump over, crashing through a jungle without paths, uphill, penetrating, hurting, squeezing a last bit of strength from an outrage that now veered into confusion as I came to a stop at the top of a small rise or hill at the foot of which lay, of all things, a lovely limpid pool or lagoon. It was idyllic down there, ordered, and tranquil.

There was a wading bird in the water. The wading bird was motionless, elegant, stylized, almost artificial, perhaps porcelain with its long slender neck and the quick hook made by its head. In fact, with its Modigliani neck, and head and bill so much in evidence—oh no: deliver me from visions, at least spare me that. I write fiction, isn't that sufficient? I turned away, squatted, sat down. I lay flat on my back. When I had my breath back I sat up and faced it directly. Goddamn, it looked like a question mark. No matter how sober I was trying to be, that made me giddy. I rubbed my eyes. My eyes blurred and that question mark of a bird shimmered.

After cleaning the scrape out and taking a drink I walked to the side of the house. I didn't feel the exertion, although by coming back for more there was no doubt I was putting some miles on this machine today. "Ain't you there yet, old buddy?" Billy asked. When I asked myself why I was going on this way, it was perfectly clear to me that I was becoming slightly unhinged, yet I suffered no loss of equanimity because of that. I could handle it, I thought, not to mention the curiosity I felt about where it would lead.

I was the fat man stuffing himself with forbidden sweets in the parking lot, the anhedoniac finally finding kicks. I was really cooking. I turned to answer Billy, who was gone.

A shrimp boat operated offshore. A yacht sailed past. An insect landed on my face. I felt my shoulder being bitten. Sweat dripped from my forehead. I was flying.

I slapped my neck and shoulder and once I started doing that I couldn't stop. I slapped my ear, my cheek. My scalp itched something awful. The only way I could slap and scratch to my heart's content was to ride without hands, which I did.

Then Dave appeared with Billy. I smacked my forehead.

"Alan," Dave said, "it's almost time for dinner."

How nice it would be, I thought, to return the favor and run him off the apron.

There was concern and authority in his voice; the tone was nothing if not fatherly.

"Don't you want to get ready?" he asked. "Everyone's downstairs."

As one well-connected uppercut will straighten even a good man up, so I was sitting posture perfect in order that I might have as much body as possible to slap.

When he took the first step toward me I moved. I dropped to the posture of a professional cyclist, wrapped my hands as tightly as possible around the handlebars, and then with a great explosion of noise yanked violently upward and backward; like a horse rearing, like a biker popping a wheelie, the front of the bike rose, he froze in midstep, the bike tottered precariously, it started to topple, and the next thing I knew I was falling, with the likelihood being I'd land not far from his feet.

ILLINOIS SHORT FICTION

Crossings by Stephen Minot
A Season for Unnatural Causes by Philip F. O'Connor
Curving Road by John Stewart
Such Waltzing Was Not Easy by Gordon Weaver

Rolling All the Time by James Ballard
Love in the Winter by Daniel Curley
To Byzantium by Andrew Fetler
Small Moments by Nancy Huddleston Packer

One More River by Lester Goldberg
The Tennis Player by Kent Nelson
A Horse of Another Color by Carolyn Osborn
The Pleasures of Manhood by Robley Wilson, Jr.

The New World by Russell Banks
The Actes and Monuments by John William Corrington
Virginia Reels by William Hoffman
Up Where I Used to Live by Max Schott

The Return of Service by Jonathan Baumbach
On the Edge of the Desert by Gladys Swan
Surviving Adverse Seasons by Barry Targan
The Gasoline Wars by Jean Thompson

Desirable Aliens by John Bovey
Naming Things by H. E. Francis
Transports and Disgraces by Robert Henson
The Calling by Mary Gray Hughes

Into the Wind by Robert Henderson
Breaking and Entering by Peter Makuck
The Four Corners of the House by Abraham Rothberg
Ladies Who Knit for a Living by Anthony E. Stockanes

Pastorale by Susan Engberg
Home Fires by David Long
The Canyons of Grace by Levi Peterson
Babaru by B. Wongar

Bodies of the Rich by John J. Clayton
Music Lesson by Martha Lacy Hall
Fetching the Dead by Scott R. Sanders
Some of the Things I Did Not Do by Janet Beeler Shaw

Honeymoon by Merrill Joan Gerber
Tentacles of Unreason by Joan Givner
The Christmas Wife by Helen Norris
Getting to Know the Weather by Pamela Painter

Birds Landing by Ernest Finney
Serious Trouble by Paul Friedman
Tigers in the Wood by Rebecca Kavaler
The Greek Generals Talk by Phillip Parotti